WORLD-EATER

On the night of the great storm, a mysterious new planet suddenly appears in the sky. Orbiting the sun between Mercury and Venus, the huge blue-grey sphere has scientists baffled as probes reveal its surface to be flat and bare and its interior liquid. Eleven-year-old Orville, absorbed in waiting for his favourite pigeon to hatch her eggs, is the first to suspect the true nature of the planet. But will anyone listen to his theory? And if they do, can they avert disaster? For if Orville is right, the world is doomed . . .

WORLD-EATER

Robert Swindells

Galaxy

CHIVERS PRESS
BATH

First published 1981
by
Hodder & Stoughton
This Large Print edition published by
Chivers Press
by arrangement with
Transworld Publishers Ltd
2002

ISBN 0 7540 6192 2

British Library Cataloguing in Publication Data

Swindells, Robert, 1939–
   World-eater.—Large print ed.
   1. Science fiction 2. Children's stories 3. Large type books
   I. Title
   823.9'14[J]

ISBN 0-7540-6192-2

Printed and bound in Great Britain by
BOOKCRAFT, Midsomer Norton, Somerset

It winged its way across the blackness of intergalactic space, searching. As it flew it scanned the void, its eye moving from gas-cloud to incandescent gas-cloud; from galaxy to galaxy.

A thousand light-years out it selected its goal, swerved and came on, heavy-laden, towards a tilted star-whorl of the third magnitude.

At first, the galaxy was a faint glowing disc but as the distance between them shrank it separated out into a million-million grains of light. The eye sifted the grains and fastened on an undistinguished fleck near the rim. The sluggish brain plotted a course-correction. The fleck grew, becoming a star. A star with nine

1

attendant planets. A star whose fate was sealed—

*   *   *

Orville came suddenly awake and lay in the dark, listening. Wind slammed across the housefront, flung a handful of rain at the window and bowled somebody's dustbin-lid away down the cobbles. There was a voice in the wind, shouting.

He scrambled out of bed and ran to the window. Mr McDougal was standing under the lamp in pyjamas, with an old raincoat about his shoulders. The wind tore at the coat and the old man was clutching it to his throat with one hand and shielding his eyes with the other, looking up at the bedroom window. He saw Orville and waved frantically. Across the road, in the garden where the pigeon-loft stood, things were flying through the air.

Orville ducked under the curtain, ran on to the landing, called his father and ran downstairs. The door was torn from his hands by the wind and Mr

2

McDougal fell into the hallway.

'The tree!' he gasped. 'It's come down on my house. The bedroom ceiling's in.' The light snapped on and Orville's father came down in his dressing-gown. 'Close the door, Orville,' he said. 'Is it bad, Mr McDougal?' The old man nodded.

'Aye. It's smashed the roof and the wind's getting under it. There's something in the sky, man; something terrible.'

Mr Copperstone frowned. 'How d'you mean: what sort of something?' The old man shook his head. 'Terrible. You canna see the stars.' Mr Copperstone took his arm and steered him into the living room. 'Sit down here,' he said. 'You've had a nasty shock. It's cloud you saw in the sky; just cloud. Clara!' He turned to call his wife, then looked down at McDougal. 'I'll take a look at your house. Mrs Copperstone'll make up a bed in the spare room and you can sit here while Orville lights the fire and makes some tea.'

Orville didn't want to light the fire or

3

make tea. He had been watching the old man; had seen him whisper 'Cloud? 'Twas never cloud, man.' His heart beat noisily in his ears and he longed to question him. His parents were talking in the hallway. When they were gone he'd do so.

He went into the kitchen and began making tea. The wind seemed to be strengthening and the house shuddered with every gust. He could feel it through his feet. When the kettle was on the gas he looked into the room. McDougal sat hunched over the gas fire. Orville went and stood by him.

'Mr McDougal?'

'Hah?' The old man turned his head sharply. His face was grey.

'What d'you think it was, in the sky?'

McDougal shook his head, gazing into the fire. 'I don't know. It was a feeling, rather than something ye see with your eyes but it was there, for all that.'

'I believe you, Mr McDougal,' said Orville. He hesitated, then said, 'I was wondering about the pigeons. The wind's awfully strong. D'you think they'll be all right?'

'Oh, aye.' The old man nodded. 'That loft'll hold, lad, never fear. Your Susie will be fine, and her eggs too.' He had helped Orville build the loft and now Susie, a hen bird he had given the boy, was sitting on her first eggs. Orville smiled, then flushed. Here he was, bothering the old fellow about a pigeon-loft when he'd just lost his home.

'I'm sorry about your house, Mr McDougal,' he said. The old man nodded. 'Aye, well; it'll mend, I daresay. Away and make the tea now.'

Mrs Copperstone came down and they sat drinking tea and listening to the wind. Presently Mr Copperstone returned.

'It's a bit of a mess,' he said, taking the tea Orville poured for him. 'I've put some plastic sheeting over the bed and I'll phone a builder in the morning. I don't know what they'll do about the tree, though. It'll take some shifting.' The old man mumbled his thanks without taking his eyes from the fire. There was a silence, except for the storm. After a while Orville got up and went through the kitchen to the back door. His kagoul hung there on a peg. He pulled it on and let himself out.

In the roaring yard he looked up. The sky was black and starless. He leaned on the wind, fighting his way to the corner of the house and down the side. Reaching the front he paused, shivering. Sheets of rain blew through orange lamplight and the wind roared in the privet hedge that separated the gardens from the road. People were out of their beds; light filtered through the curtains and fell in blurred squares on the cobbles. He dashed across to the gateway in the hedge. Inside the loft it was strangely still. Susie was sitting tight, warming the two eggs that lay beneath her. When he put out his hand she stood up and slapped at it with her wing. He spoke to her softly and she settled again, allowing him to caress her head gently with his finger. He sat on the ledge. Time passed.

The night was far gone when his father came. Going back to the house was like dream-walking. He was moving his legs but there was a force that held him back; a sucking force that threatened to pluck him from the earth and draw him away into the sky. The old man's words echoed softly in his muzzy head. 'A feeling, rather than something ye see with your eyes.' He was in the road, then there were faces and a light, and then he was in bed. He slept, and in his dream the sky was full of wings.

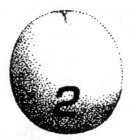

It was late when he woke up. He got up
and looked out of the window. The
storm had died down. There was
rubbish everywhere; tins and paper and
broken glass, but the loft was still
there. He dressed quickly and went
downstairs.

His mother was sweeping the step.
He stuck his head outside. 'Dad gone
to work, Mum?'

'Hours ago. It's after ten.' She went
on sweeping. It was glass, from milk
bottles.

'Where's Mr McDougal?'

'Gone to stay with his sister. Dad
took him on the way to work. Get the
dustpan, please.'

They cleared away the glass. After,

he went across to the loft. Susie was all right and the others seemed much as usual, too. He let them out to fly, fed them, then went in for some late breakfast. His mum was ironing and listening to the radio.

'Mum?'

'Ssh!' She was listening to the news. Orville shrugged and went on with his cornflakes. After a minute his mum said, 'Hear that, Orville?'

'What?'

'Listen. It says they had storms all over the world. Worse than here. Earthquakes and that. Listen.'

Orville listened, but the man was on about Bosnia. His mum made an impatient sound. 'You missed it, chomping on those cornflakes. Earthquakes and dams bursting and tidal waves and that. It's the headlines. We'll have to listen at eleven.'

'Did it say anything about what Mr McDougal saw?'

'No.' His mother's tone was scornful. 'He didn't see anything, the daft old so-and-so.' Orville sighed but did not argue. It was no use arguing.

He finished his cornflakes and got up. 'I'll have to do his pigeons as well as mine,' he said. 'They've not been fed.' He crossed to the door.

His mother shook her head. 'You and your pigeons. Why don't you go play football in the park or something, like other boys?'

He stopped, reluctantly. 'Don't like football, Mum.' He didn't like other boys much, either. They laughed at him because of his name. They laughed because of the pigeons, too.

Once, in Miss Jenner's class, he'd stood out at the front and started telling them about his pigeons. They were doing about hobbies. When he said 'Doridins', they started to titter, and when he mentioned 'Cattryses' they laughed, and big daft Cowling at the front rolled about, whooping 'Cattryses' in a high voice. Miss Jenner was blazing mad and shouted at them to be quiet. When they were, she wanted him to continue but he couldn't. He felt hot and dizzy and he knew if he tried to speak he'd cry. So he just shook his head and went back

10

to his place and sat very stiff, looking down.

Afterwards, in the yard, they got him. They crowded round him and pushed him about with their shoulders, saying 'Cattryse' and 'Doridin' and 'Pigeon-pie' until he couldn't hold it in any more and started to cry. Then they jeered and tripped him up and left him on the ground. It was a while ago now, but he still went hot when he thought of it.

'Oh, well.' His mother's voice broke in on his thoughts. 'I suppose if you were a footballer I'd grumble about your getting dirty or something. Off you go. And keep away from that tree; it's not safe.'

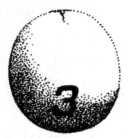

The tree had stood in Mr McDougal's garden, just inside the hedge. Now it bridged the road, its roots over a raw hole in the earth and its crown resting on what remained of the old man's roof.

Orville stood under the massive trunk, and looked up. He wondered what the bedroom ceiling was like, but the curtains were drawn across. He carried the sack of peas into Mr McDougal's loft.

He had just finished feeding the pigeons when he heard a car. The road was a dead-end and few vehicles used it. He went out and leaned on the gate.

It was a blue Simca. The driver stopped it near the top of the road and got out. He had ginger hair and a long nose. Orville didn't know him. Another man got out. He was stubby and nearly bald and he had a leather box slung round his shoulder. As Orville watched, he pulled a camera out of the box and pointed it at the tree. Longnose was writing something on a pad. Orville put down the pea-sack and went up to him.

'What are you doing, mister?'

Longnose looked at him over the pad. 'Hello,' he grinned. 'This isn't your house, is it?'

Orville shook his head. 'It's Mr McDougal's. He's gone to stay with his sister. What are you doing?'

'I'm a reporter,' said Longnose. 'Brian Fox from the *Telegraph*.' He nodded towards his companion. 'That's Dennis. He takes pictures. What's your name?'

'Orville,' said Orville. He hated his name.

'That's an unusual name,' said Brian Fox.

'I know,' muttered Orville. 'Everyone says that. When I grow up

I'm changing it to Tom.'

The reporter laughed. 'Why Tom?'

' 'Cause it's ordinary. And after Tom Bishop.'

'Who's Tom Bishop?'

'He breeds pigeons. Doridins.'

'What are Doridins, Orville?'

Orville looked at him. 'Pigeons,' he said. 'Racers. Mr McDougal says they're the best in the world.'

'Does he now? Has he got any Doridins, Orville?'

'No,' said Orville, glumly. 'And I haven't, either. They cost a lot of money. Is the tree going to be in the paper?'

' 'Spect so,' said the reporter. 'We're doing a special storm edition today. Dennis and I are prowling around, looking for interesting bits to put in.'

'D'you want to see Susie's eggs?' said Orville. 'They're interesting.'

'Susie?'

'My pigeon. One of them. She's got two eggs. They'll hatch in sixteen days' time. Shall I show you?'

'Yes, please. Just hang on while I tell Dennis.'

14

Orville took him down to the loft and lifted Susie so he could see the eggs.

'They're beautiful,' he said. 'D'you know, I'm thirty-six years old and that's the first time I've ever seen a pigeon's egg?'

Orville returned Susie to the nest. 'I'm dying for them to hatch out, Mr Fox,' he said.

'Well,' the reporter smiled. 'I expect they will, if they're fertile. How d'you tell if they're fertile?'

'They change colour,' Orville told him. 'They should be doing it any time now.'

'Oh well; good luck with them, lad. And thanks for the information.'

'Information?'

'Sure. About Mr McDougal, and the pigeons. I hope you get some of those Doridins one day, Orville. S'long!' He ducked out of the loft and went off up the road.

Orville watched over the gate as the two men drove away. Just before the car disappeared, Brian Fox waved and Orville waved back. Then he stood for a while with his elbows on the gate, thinking. Brian Fox. Now there was a man with the right name. With his long, sharp nose and reddish hair he looked like a fox. There was something foxy about his grin, too. Orville had liked him.

He sighed, turned and went back into the loft. He supposed he would never see Brian Fox again, but he was wrong.

All morning, his mother remained in a state of high excitement over the storm. As she moved from one part of the house to another she carried the radio with her. The half-hourly bulletins told of fire and flood; landslides, looting and loss of life. She listened while she prepared lunch for Orville and herself and she listened as they ate. He wanted to talk about Brian Fox but as soon as he opened his mouth she silenced him.

At five to one she switched on the TV. Nothing happened. She banged the set and twiddled the knobs. There was some crackling and a muffled voice, but no picture. Orville watched from his place at the table. The radio was still on. After a minute he said, 'You won't get it, Mum; it's just been on the tranny.'

She turned, her face pink with vexation. 'What has?'

'The news,' said Orville. 'Some masts are down and transmitters are out of action. They mentioned Lumley Moor. That's ours, isn't it?'

His mother sighed, switched off and sat down. She had waited all morning to see the news. 'Yes,' she said. 'That's ours all right. Wonder how long they'll be fixing it?'

'Dunno,' mumbled Orville, who didn't really care. 'I think Susie's eggs're changing colour.'

'What?' She stared at him blankly.

'Susie's eggs. They were white but now I think they're a bit greyish. Mr McDougal says they're fertile when they do that.'

'Oh,' said his mother, vaguely. 'That's nice, dear. Last time it was nearly a week before we got the picture back.'

'Yes,' said Orville sarcastically. 'They interfere with telly, do pigeon-eggs.'

She hadn't even heard him. He got up and went out.

They were changing colour. Susie was feeding and the cock was on the nest. Orville slipped a hand under him and brought out one of the eggs. It was definitely grey. He held it up against the light and looked at it with one eye closed. He thought he could make out a shadow inside. He held it to his ear, listening. Mr McDougal said mother birds can hear their chicks inside the egg. Orville heard nothing.

After a minute he slipped the egg back under the cock and smiled. It was alive all right and so was the other one. This time they'd hatch. He fetched his cleaning-out gear and set to work, whistling. When his dad got home at six, the loft was spotless.

There was a picture of Mr McDougal's
house in the paper, with the tree on it.
Mr Copperstone read out the bit
underneath.

'That's Brian Fox,' grinned Orville. 'I
told him what to put.'

'Good lad.' Mr Copperstone smiled.
'Doesn't say when they're coming to
shift that tree, though. Old McDougal
will be worrying himself silly.'

'They'll have hundreds of things to
clear up,' said Mrs Copperstone. 'It
could be days yet.'

'I'm just off to check the lofts,' said
Orville.

'Well, you hurry up,' said his mother.
'I've to be at work in half an hour and
you've got the tea things to do.'

His mother worked at a bingo hall in the evenings, and his dad drove her there. Orville usually washed up while they were gone.

He went up the road to Mr McDougal's. The loft was quiet. He checked the food and water and locked up, resolving to give it a good clean-out in the morning. Then he walked down to his own loft.

Susie was back on the nest. He scratched her head. 'Hello, old girl,' he murmured. 'On the night-shift, are we?' He grinned, closed up the loft and went indoors.

His parents had gone. He cleared the table, stacked the crockery by the sink and turned on the taps. He squirted washing-up liquid in the water and swished his hands in the suds. 'Fifteen days!' he whispered. 'Fifteen days tomorrow I'll have two squabs. I'll train 'em and look after 'em and do everything right and maybe they'll grow up to be racers.' He plunged a stack of greasy plates into the sink and began washing them, whistling through his teeth. If he could have known what was to happen in those fifteen days, to himself and to the world, his mouth would have been a little dry for whistling.

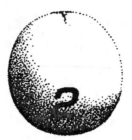

It began the next morning at breakfast.
The radio was on. Mrs Copperstone
leaned across and turned up the
volume. 'Listen!' she said. 'It says
they've found a new planet.'

Mr Copperstone lowered his paper.
Even Orville stopped eating. They
listened.

'—orbiting the sun at a distance of
seventy-eight million kilometres,' said
the newsreader. 'This places its orbit
between the orbits of Mercury and
Venus. First estimates of the object's
size put it at about two-hundred-and-
forty kilometres in diameter; about the
same as the asteroid Juno. A Jodrell
Bank spokesman has said that the new
body will probably be classed as a

minor planet, or asteroid, and that it is likely to be some time before a name is allocated to it.'

'Wow!' breathed Orville. 'A new planet. So now there's ten. I wonder what they'll call it?'

The newsreader had gone on to say that scientists were at a loss to explain where the new planet had come from. They were investigating a possible link between its arrival and the violent storms which had erupted on Earth. The object was being studied with the aid of the Hubble telescope, and an unmanned probe would be dispatched as soon as possible.

After breakfast Orville flew the pigeons and cleaned out Mr McDougal's loft. He did the job thoroughly, but a part of his mind was elsewhere. He kept thinking about the little planet. Where had it come from? Would he be able to see it at night? Perhaps there were creatures living on it, or even people. He knew that eventually they'd send a team of astronauts to take a close look and he wished he might go with them.

As he worked, he made up a story in his head. Astronauts had landed on the new planet and found that a sort of bird lived there. It was a sort of pigeon. The scientists wanted to study this pigeon, but no astronaut could be found who knew how to catch one. The ship they had was very small, so they advertised for a small pigeon-fancier and Orville got the job. Brian Fox interviewed him and Dennis took his photo. Then he squeezed into the ship and it lifted off. Landing on the new planet, he quickly trapped a couple of the pigeons and brought them back to Earth. They were green, and flew at a hundred-and-eighty miles an hour. When the scientists had finished with them, Orville got them as a reward and became the Ace pigeon-racer of the world. He was thirteen.

He finished the loft, gathered up his gear and went back to the house. His mother was waiting with some money and a list.

'Pop along to the shops for me, will you, dear?' she said. 'I've written everything down.'

25

'OK, Mum.' He took the plastic carrier, stuffed the list in his pocket and set off. It was a long walk to the shops and there wasn't much to look at on the way. He wished he'd saved the green pigeon story. Holidays were all right, but it got a bit boring and there were still fourteen-and-a-half days till the eggs hatched.

Along the street, men with brooms were clearing storm-debris, and a placard outside the newsagent's said, 'NEW PLANET—LATEST'. Orville wished something would happen.

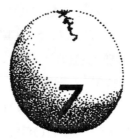

That afternoon, the telly came back on. Mrs Cashman discovered it first and went along the road telling everybody. They'd missed it so much that they all switched on, made one another cups of tea and sat watching *Playschool.* Orville fled to the loft.

At twenty-to-six his mother called him. The news was on, and there were some hazy shots of the new planet. It looked pale and smooth, but you couldn't really tell. The newsreader said an unmanned probe was on its way to do a flypast of the planet and that closer shots would be available tomorrow. Mr Copperstone missed the news but he had the paper with him and the same shots were in that.

Orville gazed at them.

'D'you think there might be life on it?' he said, thinking about the green pigeons. His father shook his head. 'No. It's not big enough. There'll be no air, for one thing.'

'How d'you know?' pursued Orville. 'Even the experts don't know much about it yet. There might be air for all you know.'

'Orville!' Mrs Copperstone frowned at him across the table. 'Let your dad get his tea and don't argue. We shall all know tomorrow, when the probe gets there. Hadn't you better see to the lofts before washing-up time?'

He sighed, put down the paper and got up. His mother was already dashing about, getting herself ready for work. He fetched the pea-sack and went out.

It was dusk. A single star glimmered in the sky. Orville stood in the roadway and searched the heavens for anything unusual. There was nothing. He shrugged and went on. Later, maybe; when it was properly dark.

The old man's pigeons bubbled softly on their perches. He checked around, wished them goodnight and locked up. His parents were getting into the car. As he walked down, it passed him with sidelights on and his father waved.

In his own loft, he topped up the feed-trough and the water container, then sat on the ledge and tickled Susie. When the light faded he got up and went outside.

The sky was full of stars. He stood on the path, gazing up at them. He picked out Orion's belt and the Great Bear, but if any one of the myriad glittering points that shone down on him was shining there for the first time, he didn't know it. He shrugged again, and moved on towards the house.

One-and-a-half thousand miles away to the east, other eyes were watching the sky. As Orville went indoors, those eyes widened and a gasp broke the silence of the tracking-station. *'Nya mozhyt bidt!'* the lone observer whispered. 'It cannot be!' She stared blankly for a moment at the banked instruments before her, then reached for the phone with a trembling hand.

While Orville was dressing the next morning, there was a knock on the front door. His father answered, and by the time Orville got downstairs the caller had gone. His father was outside, doing something to the car, and Mrs Copperstone was making toast.

'Who was at the door, Mum?'

'Man from the Council,' his mother said. 'They're coming to move the tree tomorrow.'

'Oh, great!' cried Orville. 'Why did they tell Dad?'

'Because they're closing the road in the morning. Your dad's got to have the car out by eight.'

'Oh.' He sat down at the table and reached for the cornflakes. 'It'll be something to watch, anyway; nothing interesting ever happens around here.'

'You'll keep out of the way, my lad,' his mother retorted. 'They'll not want you hanging around with that great thing to shift.'

'No, Mum.' He poured milk on his cornflakes. He'd go and watch anyway, but there was no point in arguing now. Mrs Copperstone switched on the radio.

The new planet was the main story in the news. The unmanned probe was approaching it, and had begun sending back pictures. These were being analysed, and viewers would see some of them on television later in the day. The probe was due to fly by the planet at around midday, and would eject an instrument-package which would land on the surface.

Mr Copperstone came in, and the three of them talked about the planet over breakfast. When his dad had gone to work, Orville made his mother promise she'd call him as soon as anything came on TV about it, and went out to the loft.

It was eleven o'clock when the first pictures came on. Orville ran indoors and sat crosslegged on the carpet, fascinated.

The shots began when the probe was still some hundreds of miles away from the planet. They showed a blue-grey sphere about the size of a football. As the probe flew nearer, the sphere grew on the screen until it wouldn't all fit in, and there were some close-up shots of the surface. It looked flat and bare. The commentator said it was craterless, and that scientists were surprised by this. The programme ended with a mock-up of the probe releasing its instrument-pack. It was done with computer graphics, and the Science Correspondent used a pointer to explain what was happening at this very moment, out there in space.

When it was over, Orville went back to the loft. With thirteen days to go, Susie's eggs were definitely showing dark blobs inside and he sat, scratching her head, praising her in soft, excited tones. With the new planet, and the men coming to move the tree, and

32

Susie's chicks on the way, he was
beginning to feel that the holidays
weren't turning out too badly after all.

That afternoon he walked into town and went to the library. He wanted to read about eggs; what they were made of, and how the baby birds developed inside them. Susie's eggs were a source of fascination to him; almost an obsession, and he needed to know everything about them. If Mr McDougal had been home he would have talked to him about it but he wasn't there, and nobody else was interested.

There wasn't a book about pigeons' eggs but an assistant found him one with a section on hens' eggs, which she supposed would be about the same. He took it into the Quiet Room and read for an hour. It had a lot of technical stuff in it but he managed to get a fair idea of how the eggs had been made in Susie's body, and what was happening inside them. At four o'clock he gave the book back to the assistant and set off home.

Passing under the fallen tree reminded him of tomorrow, when the men would come to shift it. It reminded him of Brian Fox, too, and on a sudden impulse he turned, went back to the main road and entered the telephone-box.

He riffled through the battered directory, lifted the receiver and dialled.

'Hello?' He pressed a silver coin into the slot. 'Is that the *Telegraph*?'

'It is,' said a woman's voice. 'May I help you?'

'Can I speak to Brian Fox, please?' said Orville.

'One moment please.' There was a buzzing noise, a pause, and a man's voice that said, 'Newsroom.'

'Is that Brian Fox?'

'Brian's out. Can I help?'

'I've got a message for Brian Fox. He

came about the tree that fell on the house. I thought he'd like to know they're coming to move it tomorrow.'

'What house, where?' asked the voice.

'Prospect Place,' Orville told him. 'They're starting at eight o'clock.'

'Aha.' The man was writing it down. 'And can I have your name, son?'

You can have it to keep, thought Orville, but he only said, 'Orville, Orville Copperstone.'

'Aha; right. I'll see he gets this as soon as he comes in, Orville. Thanks a lot. 'Bye.'

The man hung up. Orville left the box and turned into Prospect Place feeling pleased with himself.

His mother was washing lettuce. 'Where've you been?' she said. 'You've missed a good newsflash.'

'Library,' said Orville. 'What newsflash?'

'About the planet. That package is sending weird stuff back. It's hollow.'

'What; the package?'

'No!' She dumped wet leaves into the colander. 'The planet. They

36

expected a solid lump of rock or iron or something but it's not. It'll be on the telly at twenty-to.'

Orville switched on and sat on the carpet while his mother stuffed potatoes. The news opened with a close-up of the planet, and the reader said, 'Latest information from the new planet provides a surprise for the scientists.' Then he went on to read the other headlines. Orville waited, and after a few moments the reader returned to the main story of the day.

The package had landed as planned and was sitting on the surface, gathering data and transmitting it back to stations on Earth. Scientists had expected that the object would prove to be a solid mass of rock, but soundings taken by the package suggested a thin crust and a liquid interior. The crust appeared to consist mostly of calcium carbonate. The composition of the inside was as yet unknown. The whole thing, said the newsreader, was like nothing ever encountered before in the history of space exploration, and a manned flight would be dispatched to the planet within the next few days.

'What's calcium carbonate?' Orville asked, as soon as the item was finished. He'd come across it somewhere recently, but couldn't remember where. His mother shrugged.

'Dunno. A chemical, I suppose.'

'Brilliant,' growled Orville. 'I know it's a chemical, Mum; everything is.'

'No need to be rude about it,' said his mother. 'I didn't go to a comprehensive, you know. Bones are made of calcium, aren't they?'

He nodded. 'Yes. Sorry, Mum. I didn't mean to sound rude. It's just that I'd love to know, that's all.'

His mother put the potatoes on the table. 'So would we all,' she said. 'And we will, when that manned expedition gets there. I hope your dad won't be long.'

He wasn't. He strode in, tossed the paper to Orville and breathed in over the stuffed potatoes with his eyes closed. 'Hmmm!' he said. 'They smell good.' He sat down.

Orville scanned the front page. 'There's loads in tonight,' he said.

'Continued on page five, it says.'

His mother plucked the paper from his hands, smiling. 'Continued after tea, I say.' She tossed it on the sofa. They began eating.

They were halfway through pudding when Orville remembered where he had read the words calcium carbonate. He stopped chewing and glanced towards the paper. His mother looked at him. His face had gone pale. 'What's the matter, Orville?' she said.

Orville shook his head. 'Nothing. I— don't know.' He turned to his father. 'Dad: doesn't it say something in the paper about noises inside the planet; volcanic activity or something?'

His father nodded. 'I read something of the sort. Why?'

Orville stared at his plate. He was remembering Mr McDougal in the hallway, saying, 'There's something in the sky, man; something terrible.' He shivered. 'I think I know what it is,' he whispered.

His parents exchanged glances and his father shrugged faintly.

'What what is, Orville?' he asked.

39

'That planet,' said Orville. His voice was hoarse and unsteady. 'I think it's an egg.'

For several seconds, nobody spoke. His parents gazed at him, and he continued staring down at his plate.

Then his father laughed, and Orville felt a hotness that started somewhere low down and spread upwards, scalding his face. He bit his lip; fighting tears as he had on that awful day at school.

He felt his mother's hand on his. 'Orville, love,' she said. 'It can't be. Where on earth did you get such an idea from: who's been having you on, eh?'

'No-one!' He jerked his hand away and his voice cracked. His face was wet with tears. 'No-one's been having me on. I've thought about it, see? I've thought about it instead of everything going in one ear and out the other like you!' He got up so violently that his chair toppled, and he ran from the room. His mother made to follow, but Mr Copperstone laid a hand on her arm and shook his head.

'Let him go, Clara. He'll get over it better on his own.' She sank back on her chair and looked at him reproachfully.

'You shouldn't have laughed, Bob. You know how sensitive he is.'

'I know. But dammit!' His brow creased with anger. 'Where does he get his ideas from? Sometimes I swear he's barmy, that kid of ours.'

'No.' She shook her head. 'He's not barmy. He's different from other lads, that's all: more sensitive. But not barmy.'

He sighed. 'Those pigeons!'

'Well,' said Mrs Copperstone gently. 'They're his hobby. Some kids play computer games; Orville has his pigeons.'

Mr Copperstone nodded. 'Yes. You're right, I expect. I just sometimes wish he was more like I was at his age, that's all.'

'Why?' She smiled. 'What were you: an angel or something?'

'Oooh no!' He shook his head. 'Far from it. I played games, Clara. I stood on the corner with the other lads, learning to spit. I smoked on the quiet. I was a lad. I didn't spend my time thinking about the news and what goes on inside eggs.'

'You didn't spend your time thinking at all. He does, and someday we'll be glad he did: you wait and see.'

He nodded. 'All right, love. Only it doesn't do to encourage him too much with his fantasies. Eggs in space, indeed: what next?'

They returned to their pudding.

He waited in the loft till the car drove
away. Then, still burning with
resentment, he went up the road and
saw to Mr McDougal's birds.

When he returned to the house
there was a note and three pounds fifty
on the table. He read the note.

'Dear Orville,' it said. 'Get yourself a
Chinese for supper. Love, Mum and
Dad.'

He re-folded the note and put it
back on the table with the coins on top.
He didn't want their money. They'd
only left it so he'd do the washing-up.
Well: he'd do the washing-up but he
wouldn't take the money. That would
be sinking to their level. When they
came back the place would be

immaculate but he'd be in bed, asleep. They'd sense the depth of his scorn and pass a restless night, reflecting on the wrong they'd done him.

Next morning he stayed in bed till he heard his father drive off. Then he dressed and crept downstairs. His mother was in the kitchen. He crossed the room on tiptoe. The note was still on the table but the money had gone. When he didn't come down for breakfast his mother would go up. His bed was made. With any luck she'd think it hadn't been slept in. Then there'd be some fun. He let himself out and closed the door silently.

A white van was parked up the road and a policeman was putting a row of cones out. At the end a policewoman stood looking along the main road. Orville strolled across to the garden gate and went into the loft. They were obviously determined to keep sightseers away, but he'd already worked out how to get himself a grandstand seat.

There were two gardens between his own and Mr McDougal's. They were separated by privet hedges, but Orville knew places where he could get through all three of them. He'd see to his pigeons, then cross the gardens, keeping low, and let himself into the old man's loft. The loft window was only about six metres from the great, torn-out roots of the tree. He'd sit on the ledge in there and watch the whole thing and nobody would be any the wiser.

He had just put out feed when he heard the sound of a heavy vehicle. He slipped out of the loft and peered through the hedge.

A big yellow crane on caterpillar-tracks was turning into the road. It crunched and ground its way over the cobbles and the policeman walked backwards in front of it with his arms out, guiding the driver in the high cab. Behind the crane came a heavy lorry. When both vehicles were in Prospect Place, the policewoman sealed it off with cones. Orville wondered how Brian Fox and Dennis would get by.

Bent double and clutching the sack of peas, he crossed the garden and wriggled through the hedge. Mr Cashman's garden was like a jungle. He didn't even have to bend to stay hidden in it. Mr Jackson's was neat, with small new cabbages in straight rows. He scuttled across, leaving footprints, and squeezed through the privets. He was behind Mr McDougal's loft.

The policeman was busy talking with the crane-driver. Some men were unloading tools from the back of the lorry. Nobody was looking in his direction. He moved round the end of the loft, opened the door and slipped inside, closing it behind him.

The window was dusty inside and streaked with dirt outside. If he sat still, nobody would see him. He scattered some feed for the pigeons, put down the sack and settled himself on the ledge.

Almost at once, four men came through the gateway. They had spades, hatchets and a saw. Some of the roots were still in the ground, and the men dug round these so that they could be chopped or sawn off.

In a few minutes it was done. The men stood back. One scraped clay off his boots with a spade. The crane-driver called out to them and they trooped out through the gateway. A motor roared and the crane's massive boom swung round. Chains dangled from its tip. It dipped, and the chains swung against the tree. Two of the men came back and scrambled through the roots, pulling themselves up on to the trunk. They began fixing the chains. The other two appeared on Mr McDougal's roof.

Orville was so absorbed in watching these activities that it was some moments before he noticed a disturbance in the hedge directly opposite the window. When his eye was drawn to it the shrubs had parted and a red-haired man, on hands and knees, was halfway through.

Brian Fox!

Orville shot a glance towards the men on the tree. They were busy, and had noticed nothing. He got up, opened the door a crack and signalled furiously.

The reporter had his back to Orville and was helping another, heavily laden man through the gap. Orville looked again at the men on the tree. If one of them turned, Brian Fox would be seen instantly. He cupped his hands round his mouth and hissed, 'Mr Fox!'

The reporter turned, seeking the source of the voice. Recognizing Orville he grinned, raised a hand and half-dragged the hapless Dennis through the hedge. The two men got to their feet and ran, bent double, to the loft. Orville stepped aside as they piled in, then swung the door shut behind them. The pigeons fluttered in alarm.

'Were we spotted?' gasped Fox, knocking dirt from the knees of his trousers. Orville peered through the window.

'No. They can't hear for the motor.'

'Good. All right, Dennis?'

Dennis was sitting on the ledge, panting; picking bits of privet from his pullover. He grunted. Brian Fox grinned. 'Flipping policewoman wouldn't let us through,' he said. 'So we had to hop over a wall and crash through the privets. Susie OK?'

Orville smiled. 'She's fine, Mr Fox. The eggs hatch in twelve days' time.'

'Great.' He turned to the photographer. 'Better get your stuff sorted, Dennis; they'll be lifting her any minute now.'

Dennis bent by the window, fiddling with his camera. A woman's voice called out, 'Orville!' Orville ignored it, and the reporter looked at him.

'That your mum calling, lad?'

Orville nodded, scowling. 'I'm not going, though.'

'Why not?' said Fox. 'She probably thinks you're getting in the way out here.'

'No,' growled Orville. 'She thinks I've run away. Last night. She can go on thinking it for a bit, too. Serve her right for laughing at me.'

Fox grinned. 'Why'd she laugh at you, Orville?'

Orville scowled at the floor. 'I told her something; her and Dad. An idea I've got. They laughed.'

'What sort of idea?' asked Fox. 'I promise I won't laugh.'

'Yes, you would.'

'No; honestly. Try me.'

Orville shook his head and the reporter shrugged.

'OK. Suit yourself, son. An idea's got no value till it's expressed, though.'

Orville looked up. 'All right. Promise you won't laugh?'

'I already have,' said Fox. 'Promised, I mean.'

'It's about the new planet,' said Orville.

'Oh, yes?' Fox arched his brow. 'What about it?'

'It's an egg,' said Orville flatly. The reporter blinked.

'Is it? How d'you know?'

'Oh, things,' said Orville. 'Clues.'

Dennis had the door half-open and was taking shots. Orville looked through the window. The tree was clear of the ground; swinging tiltedly in its chains. Hands showed over the hedge, reaching up; trying to steady it.

'What clues?' said Fox.

Orville answered without turning. 'It's changed colour, for one thing. And it's made of calcium carbonate, same as eggshells; and it's hollow, too. And there's activity inside it, and the scientists say nothing that small has activity. It's an egg.'

'Sounds reasonable,' said Fox.

They had lowered the tree. It lay in the roadway, with some of its branches sticking into the gardens through flattened privets. Orville turned.

'You mean you believe me?'

The reporter shrugged. 'It's a perfectly sound theory,' he said. 'As good as any other. I mean; nobody knows what it is yet, so why not an egg?' He chuckled. 'There is one thing, though.'

'What?'

Fox rolled his eyes. 'If the egg's two-hundred-and-forty kilometres in diameter, how big's the thing that laid it?'

The tree finally came to rest at eight-forty-five. In Moscow it was ten-forty-five and in the room where the Government met there were some grim faces round the table.

The President gazed at them a moment, then nodded to the Secret Service man by the door. He opened the door and spoke to somebody outside. A woman entered, nervously, holding a clipboard with both hands. She lingered by the door and the President beckoned impatiently.

'Step forward,' he growled. 'Nobody's going to eat you.'

The woman advanced and stood, looking along the table.

'This,' said the President, waving a

hand in her direction, 'is Professor Valentina Petrova, of the Kamarov tracking-station near Lipeck.' He nodded to the woman. 'Present your report.'

The sixteen men round the table had been told to expect a shock, but what Professor Petrova told them in the twenty minutes that followed exceeded their wildest speculations. When it was over, the professor accepted the meeting's thanks and was escorted from the room.

The President's eyes swept the stunned faces of his colleagues. 'Well, gentlemen,' he said, 'what we have heard is Professor Petrova's theory; nothing more. But others are investigating her work and so far, everything checks.'

He made a steeple of his fingers and rested his chin on it. 'So, gentlemen; it seems we must revise our ideas about the universe and the—ah— permanence, shall we say, of systems within it. The professor stresses that, given the size of the universe, the chances of our Solar System becoming a victim are slight. Nevertheless, if her theory is correct, then at any moment the Solar System could cease to exist and there would be absolutely nothing we could do about it. In the light of this, we have to take two decisions.'

He paused, gazing into each face in turn; then continued. 'One: when do we tell the people; and two: when do we tell Houston?'

Brian Fox couldn't sleep. Ever since he had left Prospect Place that morning, Orville's words had nagged at him. It was ridiculous, of course. It had been as much as he could do not to burst out laughing when the kid said 'It's an egg.' He was obsessed with eggs, that kid.

Nevertheless, it refused to leave him alone. He had typed up the tree item, then gone through to the wireroom to see if there was anything fresh on the planet. After that he had done a tour of departments, collecting copy and proofs and a couple of back-numbers, reading and re-reading everything that had come in about the thing.

It all fitted. Everything the kid had told him was there. And yet, it was ridiculous.

Now he lay sleepless in his bed. Every time he closed his eyes he saw Orville's pale, earnest face and heard 'It's an egg' inside his skull. He groaned and looked at his watch. Eleven-twenty-five. He threw back the sheet and swung his legs on to the carpet, feeling for his slippers.

There was a man he knew; a scientist, who might be able to set his mind at rest. His name was Jim Hayle and he lived at Cambridge. Besides being a famous astronomer, Jim Hayle wrote science-fiction books. He had a taste for way-out theories about the universe and would probably enjoy this one. And, thought Fox wearily, if there was any possibility of a grain of truth in Orville's idea, then Hayle knew all the right people; he'd see that it reached the appropriate set of ears. He looked up the number, lifted the receiver and dialled, praying that the professor might be at home and not yet in bed.

His prayer was heard. Jim Hayle answered the phone himself. Brian Fox identified himself, apologized for the lateness of the hour and was invited to tell his story. The professor listened, chuckled appreciatively and told Fox to leave it with him. Fox left it with the professor and, within ten minutes, was sleeping like a baby.

*   *   *

Professor Hayle re-hung the receiver and went slowly back to his armchair. There, he sat stroking his chin and gazing into the fire. Through friends in Britain and the USA, he knew something which Brian Fox could not know. He knew that preliminary examination of the new planet was turning up data so strange and worrying that a lot of it was not being released to the press. He had put up a front for Fox, chuckling over what he had seemed to regard as material for a good yarn, but his heart had kicked within him and now, as he stared into the flames, it still raced.

Presently he grunted, nodded and stood up. It was after midnight when he lifted the phone and put through a call to Jodrell Bank.

'Orville!' Mr Copperstone came in waving the paper. Orville looked down at the table. He hadn't forgiven his father yet for laughing at him. It was shepherd's pie day, too; bad things never came in ones.

The paper landed in his lap. 'You're in the *Telegraph*, old lad,' his father said. 'Bottom of the front page.' He inhaled over the shepherd's pie and went to hang up his coat.

Orville opened out the paper and scanned the front page while his mother breathed down his neck. The main story was still about the planet. Near the foot of the page was a small item in bold print with a box round it. 'Pigeon-Boy's Egg Theory', said the headline. Orville's heart lurched. He

59

read the item rapidly.

'Orville Copperstone,' it said, 'an eleven-year-old pigeon-fancier, has come up with a startling theory about the nature of the new planet. "It's an egg," he told a staff reporter, and pointed to evidence which he says proves his theory. Orville, who lives locally, is currently awaiting the hatch of two eggs, the offspring of his favourite pigeon, Susie. Is Orville suffering from eggs on the brain, or could it be that our town has produced its own Professor Einstein: a real egg-head, in fact?'

His mother's hands smelled of raw onions. 'Here.' He thrust the paper at her. 'He's done it like a joke. Now everyone'll be laughing at me.' He got up.

'Where you going?' said his mother. 'Dinner's ready.'

Orville shook his head. 'Don't like shepherd's pie.' There was an ache in his throat. 'He didn't have to put it in the paper and he's done it like a joke. Well, he can just get flippin' lost. All of you can. I'm off to sit with Susie!' He brushed past his father and strode from the house.

$$* \qquad * \qquad *$$

As the Copperstones sat down to eat, a group of worried men and women met round another table at Jodrell Bank. Professor Gurdip Singh, the installation's Director, clasped his hands and gazed at them a moment before raising grave eyes to look at his colleagues. When he spoke his voice was calm, but the others sensed the tension underneath.

'Following Professor Hayle's telephone call last night,' he said, 'I spoke with Director Gidney at Houston. He was sceptical, to say the least; nevertheless he ordered certain tests to be carried out in the light of what I had told him. This was eighteen hours ago. Fifteen minutes ago he called back. There have been two developments. Firstly, all tests carried out so far have yielded positive results.'

There were gasps from the assembled scientists. Professor Singh held up a hand. 'I know,' he said. 'It's preposterous; impossible. And yet it's beginning to look like the truth. And secondly; something's worrying the Russians. Gidney feels they're about to hand him something through the exchange of information channel. Something nasty. He thinks it could turn out there's a connection. He's urging a press blackout on his Government and suggests we do the same.'

He paused, his eyes probing each of them in turn. When he spoke again his voice was grim.

'It is likely that over the next few days we shall receive information here the like of which the world has never known. There will be pressure from the news media for us to divulge that information, but we must resist that pressure. Nothing, and I repeat nothing, must appear in the newspapers or worldwide panic could follow. Do I make myself perfectly clear?'

'Did anybody say anything?' Orville watched his mother with anxious eyes as she unpacked the shopping. She nodded without pausing in her work.

'Oh, yes. Mrs Wallace in the breadshop. And old Stoney. They'd both seen it but they weren't laughing at you. Mrs Wallace only mentioned it so she could start telling me about when her Tracey got *her* name in the paper; she won an essay competition or something. And Stoney just said it was the only sensible thing he'd read about the planet since it happened. You worry over nothing, love.'

'Yeah.' Orville wasn't convinced. 'It's the kids, though; wait till I bump into *them*. They'll have a right laugh.'

Mrs Copperstone shut the cupboard door and hung up her bag. 'You've another fortnight's holiday yet,' she said. 'Everybody'll have forgotten about it by then; you'll see.'

'I hope so, Mum. I wish I'd never talked to that Brian Fox now. I'm just off to see to the birds.'

He did Mr McDougal's loft first, then his own. Susie let him stroke her. 'Ten days,' he whispered. 'Single figures tomorrow!' He sat by her a while, tickling her absently and thinking about Brian Fox. He still liked the reporter. Maybe he hadn't done the egg bit as a joke after all. Mrs Wallace and old Stoney hadn't taken it that way. Maybe grown-ups have a different sense of humour. He was right about the kids, though; they'd take it as a joke all right. He was glad it was the holidays. If he was lucky he wouldn't run into anyone till first day of term. By then he'd have his chicks, and maybe the kids would have something else to think about, too.

*   *   *

The Newsroom phone rang and the nearest reporter picked it up.

'Who?' He stuffed a finger in his ear and screwed up his face against the din. 'Fox? Just a minute, Mr Barnes.' He covered the mouthpiece and yelled through the smoke.

'Brian: Editor!' He waved the phone.

Brian Fox came over, took the instrument and turned his back on the room. 'Fox here, Mr Barnes.' He listened a moment, said 'Right', and dropped the phone on its cradle. The other man raised his eyebrows.

'Bother?'

Fox shrugged. 'Dunno. Soon will, though.' He threaded his way between littered desks and left the room.

There were two men with the editor. They rose when Fox entered, facing him. The editor got up, too. He looked odd.

'This is Mr Fox, gentlemen,' he said. 'Mr Fox, these two gentlemen are down from London on—ah—government business, and wish to speak with you.'

Fox grinned, nodded and stood feeling silly. His smile was not returned. One of the men waved a hand towards a third chair. 'Please.' They all sat down, and the man spoke to Fox.

'We have been talking to your editor about a very sensitive matter, Mr Fox,' he said. 'You remember this, I suppose?'

He passed over a folded copy of the *Telegraph*. Fox glanced at it. The egg item was ringed in blue crayon.

'Yes,' he said. 'I wrote it yesterday. Why?'

The man ignored his question. 'The child you interviewed,' he said. 'What's he like?'

Fox shrugged. 'A kid. Eleven. Likes pigeons. I don't know what you mean.'

'I mean, is he—bright? Would you trust him with a secret, shall we say?'

'I don't know,' Fox replied. 'I mean, I barely know him. He seems a good lad. Why?' He looked from one government man to the other; then towards the editor, who dropped his eyes.

The man regarded Fox gravely. 'Mr Fox,' he said. 'What would you say if I were to tell you that the child's theory is correct?'

Fox's mouth dropped open. He shifted his eyes to the second man, then to the editor. Nobody was laughing. He gazed at the first man. 'I'd say you were—mad,' he breathed. 'Barmy. Or setting up some sort of stunt. It's not possible.'

The government man leaned forward in his chair. 'I do not set up stunts, Mr Fox,' he murmured. 'Nor am I mad. That thing out there is an egg; and outside official circles, the only persons who know it are your two selves and this child. And believe me it has got to stay that way.'

The editor broke in. 'It's on the level, Fox. They let me check their credentials by phone before you came in.'

'But what about this?' Fox tapped the paper. 'Everyone in town'll have read it.'

The man nodded. 'Yes,' he sighed. 'That's unfortunate. Luckily, you treated the matter lightly and I fancy that, as long as no further mention is made, it will be forgotten.'

'There's one thing I'd like to know,' put in the editor. He looked at the men from London. Neither spoke, so he continued. 'That thing's two-hundred-and-forty kilometres across. If it's an egg, then—'

'What laid it?' interrupted Fox. 'That's what I asked the kid yesterday.'

The government man nodded. His pale eyes regarded them coldly through round glasses. 'We know that, too: or at least we think we do. In fact, that's why we're here. An egg by itself, even one that size, is hardly an object of terror. But let the public know it's an egg, and before you can turn round they'll ask the question you just asked. And if they don't, then the press will ask it for them.'

'Are you going to give us the answer?' asked Brian Fox.

'Yes,' said the man. 'And I'll tell you why. It's felt that, once you are fully in the picture, you will appreciate the need for absolute secrecy. Of course the whole matter is D-Noticed as of now, so you can't print anything. But we're concerned that you should not even discuss it privately with family or friends.' He nodded towards the second man. 'My colleague will give you the story, and I warn you: you had better be prepared for a shock.'

The second man was bespectacled, too. A wispy moustache adorned his lip. He held a bowler hat on his bony knees and he turned it continually in a nervous mannerism with thin, pale hands. He smiled faintly as the others looked at him and lowered his eyes, speaking to the hat as it moved in his lap, round and round and round.

'In Russia,' he began, 'there is a brilliant young physicist named Petrova. She works at a tracking-station not far from Moscow. The function of the station is to monitor satellite-launches; their own, and everybody else's. For the past few months, however, this Petrova has been pursuing some research of her own, and getting interesting results.

'On the night of the storms, she saw, or rather detected, something which seemed to confirm a theory she had formulated. She told her superiors, who told the Americans, who passed it on to us.'

Fox interrupted. 'Was it about the egg?' The man shook his head. 'Not directly. It concerned the existence in the universe of a creature so immense as to be almost beyond imagining.'

'A creature,' said the editor. 'In space?'

The man nodded. 'Yes. Of course, we're not talking about one creature; if there's one, there must be more: like the Loch Ness monsters. But unlike Nessie, this creature has never been seen, the universe is so vast that the chances of one of these things coming anywhere near the Earth are a billion to one.'

Brian Fox straightened slowly in his chair. His eyes widened. 'Are you saying that one of these—monsters laid an egg—?'

'Wait.' The man held up a hand. 'I'm

coming to that. You will recall I said these creatures have never been seen?'

Fox nodded. 'So how do we know they exist?' he said.

The man from London shrugged. 'No-one sees the wind,' he said, 'but we know it exists, because of its effects on other things. What do you know about black holes?'

Fox looked at him. 'Not a lot,' he said. 'But then, who does?'

'We do, now,' said the man, quietly. He leaned forward and his voice fell to a whisper. 'A black hole is one of these creatures feeding.'

Fox stared at the man with his mouth open while his face changed colour. 'What is this?' he croaked. 'April Fools' Day or what? Black holes suck in stars and planets and stuff. Even light. Do you expect us to believe there's a thing out there so big it eats stars? Has anybody checked on this? I mean: what do our own scientists say?'

'They seem prepared to accept the evidence,' the man told him. 'And I'm afraid we must do the same. And you haven't heard the worst of it yet.'

The reporter stared at him. 'Go on.'

'Well,' the man fiddled with his bowler, 'on the night of the storms, one of these things passed close to the Earth. That's what caused the storms. It laid an egg, which now orbits the sun. We think the sun's heat will incubate the egg, so that eventually it will hatch. When it does, there'll be a hungry chick out there. A chick that eats stars and planets and light. Tell me, Mr Fox.' He lifted his head till his eyes stared fishily into the reporter's. 'What do you suppose its first meal will be?'

'Mrs Copperstone?'

Orville's mother looked at the two men on the step, and nodded. 'Yes,' she said; her voice hesitant. 'What's it about?'

The one with the thick round glasses glanced up the road and said, almost in a whisper, 'May we come inside, Mrs Copperstone?'

The woman looked doubtful. 'Well, I don't know. I mean, are you from the Gas company or something? Have you got a card?'

The man smiled, briefly. He produced a wallet, flipped it open and held it out. 'Not the Gas company, Mrs Copperstone,' he said. 'The Government.'

'Oh.' She peered at the card behind its cracked plastic window but couldn't make it out. 'You'd better come in, then. Only you can't be too careful these days, can you?'

She stepped aside and they entered. The man put away his wallet and nodded. 'Quite right. I suppose your husband is out working?'

'Yes,' said Mrs Copperstone. 'My son's just in the shed, though. I could call him.' She was unsure of them, and meant to let them know help was near at hand.

The man smiled again and nodded. 'Yes, please. We'd like to talk to him. It's Orville, isn't it?'

'Yes.' She stuck her head through the doorway. 'Orville! Come here a minute, please.' She smiled. 'He won't be a minute. We're not in any trouble or anything, are we?'

The man shook his head. 'No, madam. We—need your help, as a matter of fact. Yours, your husband's and Orville's.'

Orville came in. When he saw the men he stopped. 'What's up, Mum?

75

Who—?'

'It's all right, Orville,' said the man in pebble glasses. 'We've come to talk with your parents and yourself, that's all.' He turned to Mrs Copperstone. 'Do you think we might all sit down?'

She flushed. 'Of course. I'm sorry. Please; wherever you like. Would you like some tea?'

The man shook his head. 'Later, perhaps; while we're waiting for Mr Copperstone to come home. In the meantime, we'd like to tell you why we're here.'

They sat down, Orville gazing with undisguised interest at the visitors' strange clothes. The man with the pebble glasses spoke, briefly and quietly. He told them that Orville's theory about the new planet was correct, but that for reasons of national security they must discuss the matter with nobody. If asked about it, they were to laugh it off as a silly joke of Orville's and talk about something else. He told them nothing about the monstrous creatures he had spoken of half-an-hour before at the offices of

76

the *Telegraph*. When he had finished, he smiled into Mrs Copperstone's pallid face and said, 'D'you think we could have that tea now, Mrs Copperstone?'

They were drinking it when Orville's father came in. He was invited to join them, and the Government man told him what he had told the others.

Later, when the visitors had gone, Mr Copperstone laid his arm across Orville's shoulders and walked with him out to the loft. 'Look; I'm sorry, old lad,' he said, awkwardly. 'I laughed at you and you were right. It goes to show: if there's something you really believe in you should stick to your guns and never mind what other folk say.' He squeezed the thin shoulder under his hand. 'Anyway; let's have a look at those eggs of yours, eh?'

When it becomes necessary to kill off a good, sensational story, the press has to have something to put in its place.

Thus it was that, while Orville's family drank tea with the two agents, the Governments of Russia, the USA and Great Britain staged an apparent disagreement over what should be done in Bosnia—a disagreement which seemed swiftly to escalate to the point where the three nations withdrew their ambassadors and issued convincing but totally spurious threats, filling the front pages of the world's newspapers with rumours of impending war. Items about the new planet shrank, retreated on to the inside pages, and ceased. Nobody noticed.

Nobody, that is, except Chris Thelwell and Toby Vance.

Thelwell and Vance wrote for a weekly magazine called *Sleuth,* whose function was to embarrass people. If the Government made a blunder, and then tried to cover it up, *Sleuth* would blazon it across the front page. If a public figure got into trouble and the newspapers missed the best bits out, you could read all about it in *Sleuth.* It was that kind of paper.

Thelwell and Vance were not fools. When the apparent crisis over Bosnia began, and the planet story died, they raised their eyebrows, exchanged knowing looks and started digging. A lot of powerful people had got together to hush something up and the pair was determined to find out what it was.

Sleuth employed a network of spies and informers, whose job it was to keep an eye on the rich and famous, and on the more interesting parts of the Government Machine. It was not long before Thelwell and Vance learned of the journey by two Secret Service agents to a small northern town on the very day that the Government killed the planet story. Their informant had followed the agents, and was able to report that they had called at the offices of a local newspaper before visiting a private house in the town.

Chris Thelwell was jubilant. 'I lived there,' he crowed. 'Years ago. Started as a cub reporter on the *Telegraph*. Have a Mintoe.'

'No thanks,' said Vance. 'So, what do we do now?'

'We go there,' his friend replied, 'and see what's cooking.' He spoke indistinctly, because of the sweet in his mouth.

Within minutes, the two journalists were strapped into a fast car, which nosed through the London traffic towards the M1. Thelwell drove and sucked while Vance stared balefully out of the window and chain-smoked a particularly vile brand of cigarette. Soon the car was filled with a bluish fug. Thelwell coughed, loudly.

'Give 'em up, Toby,' he choked. 'Suck sweets. Sweets don't give you cancer.'

'They rot your teeth, though,' muttered Vance.

Thelwell half-turned and bared his perfect teeth in a horrible grin.

'When?' he said.

In the Oval Office of the White House, the President of the United States sat behind his massive desk and gazed at his Chief of Defence. Spread between them were some satellite-photos of the egg. The President blew smoke at them.

'What would be the effect,' he asked, 'if we were to bombard this thing with thermonuclear missiles?'

'Disaster,' said the other flatly. 'The egg would be destroyed of course, but we'd create a belt of radioactive debris in orbit round the sun and spread contamination throughout the Solar System.'

The President nodded. 'Moscow's suggested we do it, and do it soon.

Remember: nobody knows when the damn thing's gonna hatch out.'

'We've got to find another way,' said the Defence Chief. 'There's got to be another way.'

'Yes I know,' said the President. 'But what? We've been into gas, poisons and high explosives. The experts rejected 'em all. That thing's getting more active by the hour and I'm sorry, Sam; I want those missiles on Red Alert and if somebody doesn't come up with something very soon I'll give Moscow the nod and fire 'em, even if it kills us all.'

Orville ran a finger down Susie's back. Only nine more days. Halfway there. At the beginning, it had seemed that this day would never come. And now that it had, there was something spoiling it. Whenever he thought of Susie's eggs now, he couldn't help thinking about that other egg. The big one.

'How big's the thing that laid it?' Brian Fox had said. Orville shivered. It had been exciting at the time; funny, even. Now it was only frightening. And the worst thing was, not being able to talk about it. The men from London must have seen Brian Fox, too. They must have told him to keep quiet about the egg, so it was no use phoning him or anything. Mum and Dad never mentioned the subject, either: at least, not when he was around. It was no fun having a secret like this one.

He sighed, picked up the pea-sack and went out. It was a sunny morning. A van was parked by Mr McDougal's house, and some men were mending the roof. He fed the old man's birds then stood by the loft and watched for a while.

On the corner of Prospect Place and the main road, somebody else stood watching. He was not interested in the roof, though. He was watching Orville. He had a black book, like the ones insurance-men carry. He pretended to be writing in it, but he wasn't. He jiggled the ballpoint-pen about and peered down the Place over the top of the book, and all the time he was sucking. Every now and then, he would put the pen in his teeth, fish in his coat pocket and fetch out a sweet. Holding the book under his arm he would unwrap the sweet, let the wrapper fall and push the sweet into his mouth. Presently, he closed the book, stretched a rubber band round it, stuck the pen down the band and walked off, leaving a snow of wrappers on the ground.

*   *   *

After tea, Orville watched his parents drive away, then went to look at Mr McDougal's roof. The men had removed most of the tiles and fitted some new timbers. The wood showed pale through the polythene that covered the hole. New tiles were stacked by the house. It would not be long before the old man came back. Orville went indoors feeling good, washed the dishes and carried his pea-sack out to the loft.

A car nosed round the corner, scrunched down the Place and drew up by the gateway. Two men got out. One went towards the loft. The other stayed by the gate, smoking.

Orville was scattering feed when a shadow crossed the window. He looked round. A man was standing in the doorway. He had thin legs, a sheepskin jacket and a corduroy cap. He smiled.

'Hello. It's Orville, isn't it?'

Orville nodded. 'Yes. D'you want me for something?'

The man nodded. 'Yes. I'm a police officer, and I'm afraid I've got some rather bad news for you.'

Orville went cold. He stared at the man. It was like a play on the telly. 'What?'

The man came forward and took his arm.

'It's—your parents,' he said. 'There's been an accident. The car. It—'

'They're dead, aren't they?' cried Orville. 'Mum and Dad are dead!'

'No, no, no!' The man seized his shoulders and shook him, gently. 'Nothing like that. Nothing half so bad. They're in hospital, but I'm sure they're going to be fine. Your mother asked for you so the doctor phoned the station. If you'd like to get your coat—'

'I don't want a coat!' There was a hard lump in his throat and a rising dread in his heart. 'I want my mum!' He broke free and made for the door. The man followed.

The second man saw them coming and got into the car. The engine roared as his colleague held the door for Orville, then slipped into the back seat beside him. It smelt funny. The car reversed at high speed up the bumpy Place and swung out on to the road. An instant's pause, and it shot forward.

Orville stared dumbly through the window. They were speeding. They'd said his mum was all right but they were in a mighty hurry to get him there. He turned, wild-eyed, to the man beside him.

'It's all right, son,' said the man. 'There's no accident. We want to talk to you, that's all. Here.' He held out a small paper bag. 'Have a Mintoe.'

The car sped southward down the motorway. A sign came up. SERVICES: 1 MILE AND 24 MILES. It was dusk.

'I want to go to the toilet,' said Orville.

'You can't,' said the man beside him. 'We'll be there soon.'

'Where?' Scared at first, Orville had grown more bold as the miles flew by. The men were ill at ease and he could feel it. They weren't murderers, that was for sure. The one in front smoked all the time and swore at other drivers, and this one chewed mints and gripped Orville's arm every time they saw a police car. He decided to make a nuisance of himself.

'Where's "There",' he asked. 'Where are you taking me?'

'Never you mind.' The man twisted his neck, looking back along the road. 'Just sit tight 'cause we're not stopping.'

'But I want to wee,' whined Orville. 'There's services in a mile.' The man gave him an exasperated look, then leaned forward and touched the driver on the shoulder. 'What d'you think, Toby?'

'No.' The other man shook his head, scattering ash down himself. 'No chance. He'd yell out or something.' He glanced at Orville in the mirror. 'Shut up, kid, or my mate'll duff you up. OK?'

Orville looked at the eyes in the glass. Worried eyes. 'OK,' he said. 'But it'll be your fault if I have an accident on this seat.' He began to squirm and wriggle; clenching his hands and looking desperate. The man beside him moved away a bit. Orville kept a straight face. They passed the service area and roared on under orange lights. He didn't need a toilet at all but it made them anxious and gave him something to do.

Time passed. He saw a sign for Hemel Hempstead. 'We're near London, aren't we?' he said.

'Belt up,' snarled the man beside him. 'And sit still.' He was out of Mintoes and in a mood.

Another sign came up. It had a six on it, and pointed to Rickmansworth and Watford. A few minutes later they left the motorway. The Mintoe-man tugged at Orville's sleeve. 'Get down,' he snapped. 'Go on: right down in the seat.' He pulled Orville down till he was almost lying, his knees pressed against the back of the seat in front. He produced a scarf.

'I'm putting this over your eyes,' he said, and he did, tying a bulky knot at the back. Orville lay there, blind and half-smothered as the car went on. 'My back's breaking,' he complained.

'Tough,' said the man.

Presently the car swung sharply left and stopped. They got out. The man held the knot and propelled Orville none too gently along what felt like a gravel path. He heard keys. The man

91

said, 'Step up,' and jerked upward on the scarf, nearly pulling his head off.

'Ouch!' yelled Orville. The other man swore, and he was pushed forward on to carpet. A door closed. Suddenly he was scared again.

'Now,' hissed a voice in his ear. 'You'll tell us what we want to know, or your mum'll never see you again.'

They sat on stools in the cramped
kitchen. Vance ground out his cigarette
in the tin ashtray and lit another.
Thelwell drummed with his fingers on
the red plastic tabletop. It was late.

'I say we should've blindfolded him
right from the start,' he said. 'There
was nothing wrong with the original
idea but we shouldn't have let him see
that Watford sign. It's too close.'

'And I say the whole thing stinks,'
snapped Vance. 'I must've been mad to
listen to you. He's had a good long
look at us and he's not thick. If we turn
him loose they'll have us within twenty-
four hours. And you called me Toby in
the car.'

'What d'you mean, "If we turn him

loose"?' Thelwell's voice cracked. 'Hey, look: we're not going in any deeper. We get the gen and then dump him near home, unharmed. You got that, Toby? Unharmed. I'm no killer.'

'I didn't say anything about killing!' said Vance quickly. 'You think I'd do that? I just wish we'd never started, that's all.'

'Well, we have,' rasped Thelwell. 'So we'd better get the information and get rid of the kid before the law arrives. C'mon!'

He stood up. Vance remained seated, gazing into the ashtray. 'S'pose he won't talk; what do we do then: torture 'im?'

'Don't talk so daft!' sneered Thelwell. 'Use your common sense, man. He's eleven and a long way from home. He doesn't know we're not prepared to do him in. He'll talk all right: wouldn't you?'

Vance drew deeply on his cigarette, plucked it from his lips and stabbed it down into the ashtray. 'OK. So let's get it over. You go first.'

Thelwell shot his accomplice a

contemptuous look and went out into the hallway.

The room was small: a boxroom really, with just enough space in it for the single bed and battered wardrobe it contained. There was no window, and the room was lit by a weak, unshaded bulb. Orville was sitting on the edge of the bed. His blindfold had been removed and he looked up as the door opened.

Thelwell entered. 'Well?' he said, sharply. 'You ready to talk, lad?'

Orville gazed at him. He felt frightened, but not as much as he imagined a kidnap victim ought to feel. There was something reassuring about a kidnapper who sucks Mintoes.

'I don't know what you want,' he said. 'I don't know any secrets or anything. I want to go home.'

'Hah!' Thelwell thrust his face close to the boy's. 'You'll go home when you tell us what we want to know. Some men from London came to your house, right?'

Orville drew back. 'N—no. I mean, I never saw any men.'

'Don't give me that!' Thelwell grabbed two handfuls of denim jacket and jerked Orville off the bed.

'They came all right and it was something to do with that planet. Now, what was it?'

Orville dangled in the man's grip, his trainers clear of the carpet, his head twisted to one side and his face red. 'I—don't know what you mean,' he gasped. 'I don't know anything about the planet, 'cept what's been on telly. What you picking on me for?'

Thelwell shook him till he gasped. 'Don't play games with me, lad. There was a bit in the paper about you. Something you said about the planet. You think it's an egg. That's what they came to see you for, isn't it?'

'No,' choked Orville. 'No, it isn't. That was a joke. I said it as a joke and they put it in the paper. I can't breathe!'

Thelwell turned his fists, tightening his hold. 'They called at the newspaper office and they called on you and then it all went quiet,' he snarled. 'We want to know why!' He flung the boy on to the bed and stood panting, his red face damp with sweat. 'And you'll stay here till you tell us, or till we lose patience and throttle you. It's up to you, lad!' He turned to Vance, who had remained in the doorway. 'Tie him!' he snapped.

In two minutes it was done. They went away, leaving him to sit twistedly, his wrists tied with clothes-line to the bed. He felt sick, and far more frightened than before. He tried thinking of heroes he'd read about who refused to crack under interrogation but it was no use. He didn't feel heroic: only sick and scared.

He struggled a while against the rope but only succeeded in hurting his wrists. If there had been a window he might have tried shouting, but he guessed that they'd have gagged him if there was anyone to hear. There was no traffic noise; no footsteps. This house must be somewhere lonely. He shivered.

For a time he could hear the men's voices downstairs, and the occasional scrape of a chair. Presently the house grew silent and he slept, half-sitting; to

dream of giant eggs and Mintoe-men
and feathers in the wind.

'Well, I thought it was Mr Copperstone coming back like he sometimes does at that time so I didn't take much notice till it started making that racket and then I looked through the curtain and there it was going backwards like a scalded cat and I thought—'

'Mrs Cashman.' The detective-sergeant raised a hand to stem the flow and the woman broke off, hurt. 'Mrs Cashman: can you tell us what make of car it was?'

'Blue.'

The constable behind her caught his superior's eye and grinned. 'Make,' repeated the sergeant, patiently. 'Do you know what make it was, madam: was it a Ford, for instance?'

Mrs Cashman looked blank. 'Oh, I've no idea, love. They all look the same, don't they? Could've been a Ford, I suppose. It was definitely blue, though.'

'Yes; I've got that. I suppose you didn't get the registration number?'

'I told you; it was going very fast.' She sounded indignant.

'Quite. And how many people were in the car, Mrs Cashman?'

'There was three,' said Mrs Cashman firmly. 'Definitely three. There was the driver. 'E was in front.'

The constable smirked again and the sergeant shot him a crushing glance.

'Then there was little Orville of course, and this other chap in a cap. Stiff.'

'Stiff?'

'Yes. You know.' She searched for an alternative word. 'Nearly as wide as 'e was high, like.'

'Oh, I see.' He avoided the constable's gaze. 'Stocky, thick-set. Is that it?'

She nodded, smiling. 'That's it, Sergeant; stiff.'

When Mrs Cashman had closed her door behind them the constable looked sidelong at his companion.

'So that's it then, Sarge,' he said. 'Easy. We're looking for a blue car with the driver in front. Can't be many of them about.'

'Don't be flippant, lad,' said the detective, wearily. 'This is a serious matter. Government's involved in it somewhere, though I'm blowed if I know how. Hell of a panic on, though. Seems these so-and-sos have nabbed the kid for some information he's got, and if we don't get 'im back before he tells 'em—' He shrugged. 'God knows what might happen.'

They passed through the halo of the street-lamp and merged into the night, their footfalls fading. Behind the Copperstones' window somebody was weeping. Pigeons bubbled softly in the dark.

Brian Fox locked his car, crossed the road and stood with his hands in his pockets, looking down Prospect Place. There was a van outside the old man's house. Its rear doors were open. A youth in spattered overalls pulled out a paper sack and tottered with it into the house.

Fox strolled down between the van and the wrecked privet where the tree had fallen. Bark, twigs and dirt still littered the cobbles, criss-crossed with tyremarks. He looked down at these. One set had been made by the kidnappers' car. He knew the police had examined every inch of ground. He knew they had gone through the houses and dusted for prints in the pigeon-loft. They had done everything they could and had found nothing. It was daft to think he might turn up something they had missed, but he had come anyway. That Orville was a nice kid.

He walked down to the Copperstones' house and looked through the gateway in the hedge. Pigeons called from the loft and he wondered if anyone had fed them. He looked down. Tufts of dewy grass grew in the gateway. Yesterday somebody else had stood where he was standing but the ground between the tufts was hard and there were no footprints.

Absently, he hacked at a clump of appleweed with the side of his shoe. Down among the feathery leaves lay a tiny ball of paper. He bent and picked it up, plucking at it till it opened out into a crinkly rectangle with red lettering on one side. He lifted it to his nose. There was a faint, minty smell.

He stood with narrowed eyes, holding the wrapper in his palm. Anybody seeing him would have sworn he was deep in thought, and they would have been right. Presently, he slipped the wrapper into his pocket and walked slowly back up Prospect Place, looking at the ground. On the corner where the bogus insurance-man had stood were four more wrappers.

He squatted and picked them up, watched by two grave-eyed little girls. As he straightened up, one of them said, 'What you doing, mister?' Her companion slapped her, giggling, and said, 'Sarah!' Fox grinned.

'I save sweet-wrappers,' he said. They gazed after him, pityingly, as he walked away towards the telephone kiosk.

He lifted the receiver, called *Sleuth* magazine and asked for Chris Thelwell, who had worked with him years before on the *Telegraph*. The girl was sorry; Mr Thelwell was not in the office. Did he wish to speak to somebody else? Mr Vance? She was awfully sorry, but Mr Vance was not available either. When were they expected back? Nobody knew, exactly; they were out on an assignment and might be gone several days. Could she help? Fox told her she already had, and hung up.

He left the kiosk, sprinted to his car and drove off at high speed in the direction of the motorway.

A black limousine turned into Downing Street and stopped in front of Number Ten. The handful of sightseers which seems perpetually to occupy the pavements thereabouts closed in, agog to identify the passenger.

The Foreign Secretary slid out, muttered something to the chauffeur and moved briskly up the steps, acknowledging the salute of the constable there with an inclination of his head before disappearing inside. The sightseers resumed their vigil.

The Prime Minister rose to greet him, invited him to sit, and resumed his own seat behind the desk. There were no preliminaries. Crisply, he outlined the facts he had gleaned from the morning's dispatches. They were depressing.

Instruments monitoring the egg detected rapidly strengthening activity within. The Russians, anxious to launch nuclear missiles at it, were champing at the bit over the USA's insistence on exploring all other possibilities first. The disagreement was casting a perceptible chill over relations between the two, and with nuclear warheads potentially involved, the situation was highly dangerous. One of a handful of private citizens privy to the truth had been abducted, and those whose job it was to monitor public opinion had detected a groundswell of suspicion at the way in which the news about the new planet had dried up.

The Foreign Secretary was to speak by telephone to his opposite number in Washington, then fly to Moscow to try to persuade the Russians to hold back. Meanwhile, here at home, troops would be put on standby to deal with the mass panic which would follow if the nature of the crisis became known to the public, and the Civil Defence Corps would move quietly to action stations in case fallout from a nuclear assault on the egg threatened large-scale contamination.

The sightseers, coatless in the sunshine, nudged one another as the bespectacled statesman re-emerged. They watched, grinning self-consciously, as he got into his car and was driven away.

They lingered, smug and happy on the warm flagstones, beneath a sun whose warmth they never dreamed might soon unleash annihilation.

'I haven't had a good night, kid, so
don't mess me about. What did those
men say to you?' Thelwell stood in the
doorway. His shirt was rumpled and his
hair uncombed. Downstairs, someone
was frying bacon.

Orville looked at the man, then
down at the worn carpet. 'I'm hungry,'
he mumbled. 'And I'm cold and I want
to go to the lav.' He jerked against the
cord that bound him to the bed. 'This
hurts.'

Thelwell tossed the tie he'd been
holding on to the bed and bent, tugging
at the knots. 'OK,' he grunted. 'Go to
the toilet. But there's no breakfast till
you tell me what I want to know.' The
cord slipped. Orville freed his hands

and stood up.

'Where's the lav?'

Thelwell nodded to the landing. 'Down there. Last on your left. And don't try anything funny 'cause I'm not daft, lad.'

He walked stiffly down the landing. Even his face felt stiff. He used the lavatory, then bent over the washbasin and splashed some cold water on his face, rubbing his eyes. Turning, he pulled a towel from the rail. There were red lines on his wrists with bluish, puffy edges. He dabbed his face with the towel. At home, his mother would have called up to him at least a couple of times by now to say that his breakfast was going cold. Numbly, he wondered what she was doing this morning and then, before he knew it, he was crying. It was not fear that made him cry. It was rage. His fists screwed up the towel as he cried into it through bared teeth. He knew what his mother would be doing: she'd be crying, that's what. Dad would be off work. They'd be worried sick, imagining him dead somewhere. And it was all *their* fault:

that Mintoe-sucking git on the landing and the other one downstairs.

He flung the towel aside and ran back along the landing. Thelwell caught his flailing arms and wrestled him down on to the bed. He writhed and kicked, making harsh noises in his throat. The man flung up a knee to pin his legs and tightened his grip on Orville's wrists till the boy subsided, gasping. He twisted his head to one side. 'You git!' he choked. 'You rotten git. My mum's worrying herself to death because of you. Let me go home, you stupid slob!'

Thelwell laughed. 'Oh, so that's it! Well, you can go home whenever you want, lad,' he said, without relaxing his grip. 'All you've got to do is talk and we'll have you there in a jiffy.'

'I can't!' His voice cracked. 'They told me to say nothing. They'll lock me up if I do. Let go of me, you slob; you're hurting!'

'All right.' Thelwell let go and stood up, retrieving his tie. 'I'll go. But you stay there and think about your mum. I'll be downstairs when you're ready to talk. Just give us a yell. OK?' He turned and walked out, knotting the tie as he went.

Orville sat up, wiped a sleeve across his cheek and stared at the floor. His rage was spent but he was filled with a sort of cold anger. His mum and dad were decent folk. Why should they suffer because of rubbish like those two downstairs? He slammed his fists down on his knees. They could do what they liked: anything. He'd tell them nothing.

Vance turned as Thelwell entered the kitchen. 'Has he talked?'

Thelwell shook his head. 'Not yet. He will, though. He's upset about his mum.'

Vance shovelled bacon on to two plates and banged them down on the table. 'You're barmy, Chris,' he said. 'He's had all night to think things over and he still isn't talking. Can't you see he's not going to?'

'Sure he is.' Thelwell sat down and poked a greasy rasher with his fork. 'Where's the eggs, old son?'

'There are no eggs!' flared Vance. 'Listen. I've had enough of this. I never closed my eyes last night listening for the police. Let's dump the kid, Chris: it's getting too big!'

'No.' Thelwell filled his mouth with bacon and prodded the air with his fork. 'He's getting hungry and he's thinking about his mum. He'll crack. We've come this far, Toby; let's not throw it all away for the sake of half-an-hour.'

Vance gave a sceptical grunt and turned his attention to his plate. They ate in silence.

*　　　*　　　*

Brian Fox kept his foot down, doing seventy. The rising sun burned sullenly over fields to his left. It was a long shot, he told himself. A series of long shots in fact; but they added up to something worth chasing. He went over it all for the tenth time as he drove.

One: somebody had kidnapped the kid, Orville.

Two: his people were not rich, so it hadn't been done for money. And besides, it was too much of a

113

coincidence that he should be taken now of all times, when he had a dangerous secret to keep. So: he'd been kidnapped for information.

Three: who could use the information, with a Government ban on publication? Answer: someone who didn't give a damn about the Government ban; somebody from the alternative press, perhaps.

Four: Mintoes. Somebody had hung about the top of Prospect Place eating Mintoes. The same person had probably thrown down a wrapper by the Copperstones' gate.

Five: (and this was the clincher as far as Fox was concerned) who eats Mintoes and writes for the alternative press?

Answer: Chris Thelwell, one-time reporter on the *Telegraph* and colleague of Fox. Colleague, not friend; for Mr Thelwell was not a very nice guy, even in those days. A bit ruthless, he was; the sort of fellow who might kidnap a kid to get a story, in fact.

And lastly: if it *was* Thelwell, where would he have taken the kid? Perhaps to the weekend cottage he'd boasted of once on a flying visit to his old place of work. The cottage was at Chipperfield, near Watford. And who co-owned it with Thelwell? None other than one Toby Vance, currently absent from his desk at the offices of *Sleuth*.

Fox smiled grimly. A shaky story, but one which hung together and rang true. He hit the outside lane, passed a string of trucks and roared on, burning up the road.

'Chris; c'mere quick: there's something wrong with the kid!'

Vance had gone up with the idea of frightening the boy, and had found him lying on the bed. His eyes were half-closed, his breathing rapid and his limbs twitched spasmodically.

Thelwell came bounding up the stairs and the two of them gazed at Orville from the doorway. He twitched and groaned. Vance rounded on his partner. 'What d'we do now?' he cried. 'He's sick and we can't even get a doctor. We'll wind up with a body on our hands and it's all your fault!'

'Shut up.' Thelwell thrust him aside, bent over the bed and laid a hand on Orville's forehead. 'What's up, lad?' he said. 'Are you hot; d'you feel sick or what?'

Orville rolled his eyes up into his head and mumbled something through dry lips. Thelwell bent closer. 'What?' He shook the boy's shoulder. 'Did you say something, lad?'

'In,' whispered Orville, straining to speak. 'In—in—'

Thelwell's ear practically touched the boy's mouth. 'In what, lad?' he breathed.

'Injection,' croaked Orville.

Thelwell sprang erect and turned. 'He's saying injection.' Vance paled. 'That's all we need,' he babbled. 'He's one of those kids who needs an injection every day: insulin or something. I'm off!'

Thelwell's eyes widened. 'Here: you can't run off and leave me with this lot. What if he dies?'

'Tough. He should've talked, then he'd be home by now. Leave 'im, Chris!'

'Just a minute!' Thelwell grabbed the other man's sleeve. 'We can't leave him here, you twerp. It's our place,

117

remember? We've got to get him out; take him to a hospital or something.'

'No way!' Vance broke free. 'You take him to hospital and there's another bunch of people who can identify you. Get him in the car and we'll dump 'im by the roadside.'

'He'll die, Toby.' Thelwell's eyes were wild. 'He needs help.'

'So much the better,' snarled Vance. 'Let him die, as long as he does it somewhere else.'

'That's it, you heroes,' grated a third voice. 'Leave the kid to die!'

The pair spun round. Brian Fox stood in the doorway with his fists clenched.

'Fox!' Thelwell's eyes bulged. 'How the—?'

'Brian!' Orville sat bolt-upright, shot off the bed and barged between his captors. Fox caught him in the crook of an arm. 'All right, Orville,' he said. 'You're OK now. Did you tell 'em anything?'

'No, Mr Fox; nothing.' He held on to the reporter's jacket and gazed at the stunned pair. Vance sank on to the bed but Thelwell advanced, his mouth warped with fury.

'I'll flamin' kill you, you little sod!' he snarled.

'Watch it!' Brian Fox thrust the boy behind him and raised his fists. 'I'd love to smash most of your face in, Thelwell,' he hissed. 'Just give me the chance, eh?'

Thelwell stopped. He was neither particularly fit nor particularly brave. The two glared at each other for several seconds, till Thelwell dropped his eyes. 'What you going to do, Fox?' he mumbled.

'That depends,' said Fox. 'I ought to turn you in for abducting this kid. You'd come out a wreck, Thelwell; they don't like your sort in prison. But I'll do you a favour if you've the sense to take it.'

'What sort of favour?' Thelwell's voice was sullen.

'Leave the country,' said Fox. 'Now, tonight. I'll tell the police you'd gone when I arrived. But if I ever see either of your names on a byline again, if I even hear that you're in the country I'll shop you. Right?'

'Take it, Chris,' growled Vance. 'We've no choice.'

Thelwell gazed wretchedly at Fox. 'I've a house,' he whispered. 'Furniture. A car. Money in the bank. I've worked twenty years to get where I am and you stand there and tell me to throw it all away?'

The reporter shrugged. 'Suit yourself, Thelwell. If I turn you in, it'll all be waiting for you when you come out.' He grinned, wryly. 'What's left of you. Now; make your mind up: which is it to be?'

Toby Vance stood up. 'I'm off,' he said. 'You please yourself, Chris.' He brushed past Fox. Thelwell gazed after him, then back at Fox.

'I'll have you, Fox,' he said. 'I don't know when or how but I'll have you one day when you're not looking.' He sounded close to tears and, as he pushed past, Fox seized his lapel and grinned into his face.

'Mintoes!' he said.

Susie was dead.

Brian Fox had delivered Orville to his parents and gone off to inform the authorities. The reunion had been joyful but when his father had told him about Susie he had broken from them and gone running out to the loft.

Somehow a cat had got in. Nobody knew how, but when his father had opened the door that morning it had dodged through his legs and Susie was dead on the floor.

She was still there. In a corner a second bird lay dead. The other pigeons flew up as Orville entered, then perched nervously, watching him. The eggs were cold and he knew they were dead. He squatted by Susie's body, holding them in his hands. Susie's breast-feathers were damp little points from the cat's saliva.

Later, two policemen in civilian clothes came to the house. They took Orville into the front room by himself and asked him a lot of questions. He lied to them for Brian's sake, saying his captors had fled at the sight of the reporter's car. He didn't understand why Fox had let them go, and he was unhappy about the lie.

In the evening, Brian called to see if he was all right. Brushing aside the Copperstones' expressions of gratitude he sat with them, drinking tea and talking. It was past Orville's bedtime but nobody mentioned it. They talked of this and that while the boy gazed morosely into the empty hearth, thinking about the eggs that lay useless on the window-sill in his room. They did not talk about the awful secret they shared but it was there; binding them together and setting them apart from everybody else.

It was nearly eleven when Fox looked at his watch, uttered an expression of surprise and left, shaking his head at their renewed thanks and apologizing for the lateness of the hour.

Orville thought that he would never sleep for the turmoil inside his head but he slept, deeply and at once so that his parents, looking in a moment later, smiled and went away.

He buried Susie in a disused bit of garden beside the loft. She was light and stiff. He laid her on her back with the two eggs beside her. He was crying, but soundlessly. When he scraped the earth back into the hole it was like blotting out all the hope and excitement the holidays had begun with.

Friday. Two more weeks and he'd be back at school. 'And what did you do in the hols, Coppers?' somebody would ask. 'Race your Cattryses, did you; and your Doridins?' There'd be a ring of malicious faces round him and somebody, daft Cowling probably, would ask, 'Did you beat 'em, Coppers?' and they'd all collapse laughing. It was the oldest joke in Europe but it still got them falling about and laughing in their forced, raucous way.

'I was kidnapped.' That would shut them up. 'I was held captive in a house near London by two ruthless spies who wanted some top-secret information from me. They tied me up and threatened to kill me but I didn't talk. They'd have done me in for sure, only I was rescued in the nick of time.' They'd stop laughing then, all right.

The trouble was, he couldn't do it. There'd been no reporters when Brian brought him home, and no photographs. No story of his abduction had appeared in the papers. Even Mrs Cashman had been left guessing. The secret was still a secret. He'd had the biggest adventure of his life and nobody knew.

He hated the secret. He was fed up with it. He'd always been a loner but this thing seemed to isolate him more than ever. He dreaded meeting people in case they mentioned the egg thing in the paper. He hoped the kids had forgotten about it, or better still, had missed it altogether.

His mum hadn't asked him to run down to the shops today. She kept coming out and asking if he was all right. She seemed to be expecting more kidnappers any minute and when a car turned into the Place she was there like a flash, on the step, wiping her hands on her pinnie.

It was a taxi. It lurched over the uneven cobbles and stopped by Mr McDougal's house. The old man got out and stood, looking up at his roof. The taxi reversed noisily, swung out on to the main road and roared away. Mrs Copperstone caught the old man's eye and waved. McDougal nodded, smiling through his whiskers. Then he fumbled in his jacket pocket, produced a key and let himself into the house. Mrs Copperstone crossed to the gateway.

'Orville?'

'Yes, Mum.' He came from behind the loft, wiping his eyes with his sleeve.

'Mr McDougal's back.'

Orville smiled wanly. 'Can I go up and see him, Mum? I've got to tell him his birds are all right and that.'

'Well; I'd wait a bit, I think,' she said. 'Give him a chance to get his breath. I'll make him some tea soon and you can take it to him if you like. All right?'

He nodded. 'OK. I've—buried Susie.' His voice wavered and his mother laid an arm across his shoulders, propelling him gently towards the house. 'I know, love. Try not to fret. Your dad and I'll get you another just like her and there'll be more eggs before you know it.'

'Yes.' He knew she meant well but she was wrong. There wasn't another like Susie, anywhere. Susie was special. He bit his lip to keep from crying again.

Twenty minutes later he carried a mug of tea up to Mr McDougal's house and talked to him while the old man drank. He told him about Susie, leaving out the kidnapping, and assured him that his own birds had been cared for and were fit. The old man's eyes smiled at him over the rim of the mug.

'You've done a fine job, laddie,' he

said. 'As I knew you would. We'll raise you another hen so don't go grievin' for old Susie. When you've had pigeons as long as I have you'll know that they come and they go.' He drained the mug and set it on the table, wiping his mouth with the back of his hand. He grinned, suddenly.

'What was that I read in the paper about you: something about this new planet being an egg? Was that a joke or what?'

Orville went cold. He had to force himself to return the old man's grin.

'Yes,' he said. 'It was a joke.' He yearned to tell the truth; to share his burden with the kindly old fellow but instead he had to lie. He wondered if it showed, because Mr McDougal was looking at him oddly.

'It's a queer sort of a joke, that,' he said. 'Whose idea was it, son?'

'Brian's.' He had blurted the first name that came into his head. This was the first time he'd been confronted about the egg story and he knew he wasn't doing very well.

'Who's Brian?' A small frown had

appeared between the old man's eyes and he was sitting forward in his chair. Orville felt his face burning.

'Brian Fox,' he said. 'He's a reporter. He came to take a picture of your house and I talked to him and then we made up this story.'

Mr McDougal's frown deepened. 'But why, Orville?' he asked. 'It's not the sort of thing the *Telegraph* goes in for. Did they pay you for it or what?'

'No.' Suddenly he knew that if the old man pursued this any further he wouldn't be able to stand it. He'd break down and tell him everything. He reached for the mug.

'If you've finished with this I'd better go,' he said desperately. 'Mum told me to come straight back.'

Mr McDougal's hand shot out, closing on his wrist. The pale old eyes gazed into his own. 'Something's wrong, son. I can tell. D'you want to talk about it?'

'No! No I can't.' He rotated his wrist to break the old man's hold. It gave, too easily. His hand flew up and the mug crashed to the floor. For an instant he remained, staring down at the pieces. Then he turned and ran from the house.

'I've got to talk to you, Mr Fox. If I
don't, I'm going to tell someone about
the egg, 'cause I can't stand it any
more!'

The line crackled and he could hear
someone typing. Fox's voice was low
but emphatic. 'Not a word, Orville; not
to anyone. I'm tied up right now but I'll
come over as soon as I'm free. Just
hold on lad; OK?' The line went dead.

Orville hung up, turned and pushed
open the stiff door of the kiosk. His
hands were shaking and he felt sick. He
walked slowly back into Prospect Place
and down to the loft.

He sat on a ledge, staring blankly at
the floor while the pigeons cooed softly
around him. There were broken peas

and bits of grain in the seams between the planks. The place smelt. It needed a good clean and the birds ought to be flown but he couldn't face the work. He sat with his hands in the pockets of his jeans and his feet crossed, waiting for Fox. The feeling of sickness passed but his limbs shook at intervals and his mood fluctuated between periods of blankness and the verge of tears. When the reporter came he broke down.

Brian Fox, self-conscious in the semi-darkness, sat beside him till the spasm passed, then lent him a handkerchief. 'It's all right, lad,' he said. 'It's the shock, I expect: what they call delayed reaction. It's not every day a man gets kidnapped. You'll feel better in a bit.'

Orville mopped his face and blew into the handkerchief. He felt daft.

'I'm sorry, Mr Fox,' he said. 'I didn't mean to start crying, only I feel rotten and I keep thinking about Susie and the space-egg and that. I wanted to talk to someone.'

'Well.' Fox shrugged and grinned. 'Here I am. And not so much of the

"Mr Fox". The name's Brian. OK?'

Orville attempted to smile. 'OK.' There was an awkward silence, broken when they both began speaking at once. Fox laughed and said, 'No: go on. You were the one that wanted to talk.'

'I feel scared,' said Orville. 'And I wondered if you did, too. When they had me in that house I had a dream about the egg. It was horrible, and I had another last night. I can't stop thinking about the sort of thing that laid it. What d'you think it's like, Brian?'

Fox sat silent, his eyes on the floor. He knew what it was like. He also knew that he must keep the knowledge to himself. Presently he shook his head. 'I don't know, Orville; but I keep thinking about it too, so I know how you feel. They'll tell us, I expect, when they want us to know.'

'What d'you think they're doing, though?' pressed the boy. 'They must be doing something, mustn't they? Why don't they want people to know?'

The reporter shrugged. Orville, he sensed, was nearing the end of his

133

tether. The lad knew only half of the story and could see no reason for all the secrecy. If he was to remain silent, he needed more information; something which would impress on him the necessity for silence. Praying that his action was the right one, Brian Fox gave it to him.

'Listen, lad,' he whispered. 'The scientists have a pretty fair idea what's inside the egg, and it's something that threatens the whole world. Right now they're working on ways to destroy it before it hatches. If the story gets out before they succeed, there'll be worldwide panic. It's up to us, you and me, to buy them the time they need by keeping quiet. D'you see now?'

Orville gazed at the reporter through haunted eyes. 'Yes.' He shivered, frowned and bit his lip. 'But why can't they destroy it, Brian? It's just an egg. They've got missiles that can blow up whole cities. Why don't they bomb it, quick, before it hatches out?'

Fox shook his head. 'I don't know, Orville. They'll have thought of that. There must be reasons why they don't do it. Maybe it's because those things spread contamination over millions of miles. I just don't know.'

The boy shivered again. It had been there all the time, of course, at the back of his mind; fermenting nightmares and casting a shadow over everything else. But now that he was actually talking about it, it suddenly came real for him. He had thought it would make him feel better to talk but he felt worse.

'It really is out there,' he whispered. 'I was the one who said it was an egg, wasn't I, Brian? They didn't know, did they?'

The reporter shook his head. 'No.'

'Well, I wish I hadn't!' He pushed himself erect and stared through the window. His voice shook. 'I wish I'd kept my mouth shut. If you hadn't put that in the paper about me I wouldn't have been kidnapped and Susie would be on her eggs and everything'd be like it was!' He spun round, his face contorted with sudden fury.

'What you sitting there for, eh?' he yelled. 'Why don't you sod off, Brian,

135

now that you've messed everything up? Why don't they make that cowing egg go cold like my eggs went cold: it kills 'em, y'know!'

In the face of the boy's verbal assault, Fox had lowered his gaze. Now his head jerked up and he leapt to his feet, one hand raised.

'Hold it, Orville!' he cried. 'What was that you said?'

Orville took a step back. 'I said why don't you sod off,' he snarled. 'And I meant it, too. Sod off!'

'No.' The reporter shook his head. 'Not that. You said something about the egg.'

'They knew how to kill mine, didn't they?' Orville was cooler now, his tone truculent. 'Why don't they make this one go cold too?'

'That's it!' Fox's eyes held a manic light and he slammed a fist into his palm. 'By heck; I bet they never thought of it. Hey, listen!' He seized Orville's shoulders. 'I'm off to call Hayle. Wait here. I bet you've done it again!' He turned, striding towards the door.

Stung by the man's indifference to his rage, Orville called after him, derisively, 'What you gonna do, Brian; turn off the sun?'

'Hello?' A lorry thundered past. The reporter stuck a finger in his ear and twisted up his face. 'Is that Professor Hayle's residence?'

A quacky 'Yes' broke through the static, followed by something he didn't catch. He crouched with his back to the road. 'It's desperately urgent that I speak with the professor.' He tried to speak distinctly, screwing up his eyes against the crackle.

'Speaking.' The crackling ceased, abruptly, and Fox realized that he was bellowing.

'Professor Hayle?'

'Yes.' The professor sounded pained. 'Only please don't shout, old chap: they invented this blessed instrument so that there'd be no need to shout, y'know!'

Fox grinned briefly. 'It's Fox here,' he said. 'I've been talking to that kid again.'

'Kid?'queried Hayle. 'Oh, you mean Orville, the boy genius?'

'Yes. You're not going to believe this, but he's come up with another bright remark.'

'Good Lord! What is it this time?'

'He says: "Why don't they make the egg go cold?" '

'Why don't they make—' Hayle's voice tailed off. There was a long silence. Fox looked out through the kiosk window, glanced at his watch and said, 'Hello?'

Hayle responded at once. 'Sorry, Fox. Listen. I think he may have something. I'm going to pass it on. I must ask you to hang up now so that I can do so. I'll call you later at your home. All right?'

'Right!' said Fox. The professor hung up. Fox dropped the receiver into its cradle and left the kiosk.

*   *   *

'A shield?' The Prime Minister raised his eyebrows. 'What exactly do you mean, Professor?'

Hayle leaned forward in his chair. He had been whisked to London so quickly his head was still spinning.

'A shield of metal, sir; between the egg and the sun. Built from debris already floating around out there; boosters and fuel-tanks and so on. I believe it can be done.'

The Prime Minister eyed him shrewdly. 'But surely such a shield would have to be very large: many kilometres in diameter. Is there really that amount of material available?'

'Yes, sir,' Hayle nodded. 'Solar-panels would make up the biggest part of it. There's just about enough, I'd say.'

The man nodded. 'And how would you get it all into position?'

'We'd tow it, sir,' replied Hayle. 'As you know, in weightless conditions one shuttle can pull an enormous load. The Americans have more than forty shuttles available and Russia has nine.'

The Prime Minister nodded. 'Would it work, Professor?'

'I believe so, sir. The thing inside that egg needs warmth. The shield would keep the sun's heat from it and that ought to prove fatal. But we've got to hurry, sir. If the creature hatches before we get to it—'

'Quite.' The Prime Minister thought a moment, then picked up one of the three phones on his desk.

'Get me Washington,' he said. 'Priority.' His eyes met Hayle's. 'Leave me now, Professor Hayle,' he said. 'I think I can promise you that things will begin to happen quite quickly.'

*   *   *

The Oval Office was blue with smoke. The President had been there all night. He leaned forward and gazed at his Chief of Defence through red-rimmed eyes.

'Sam,' he said. 'Houston just called. Activity inside that goddam egg's increasing. They estimate it'll hatch inside of forty-eight hours and that's just an estimate: it could be way out either way. I've called Moscow. Told 'em we do it their way. We launch in two hours' time.'

'Two hours?' The Defence Chief paled. 'What about the fallout, Mr President? Contamination?'

The President moved his hand impatiently. 'To hell with all that, Sam: we've gotta go and you know it. If we don't act now—'

The intercom buzzed. The President flicked a switch. 'I said no calls, Mary,' he rapped.

'I know, sir.' His secretary sounded tired. 'It's London. Priority. I think we better take it, sir.'

'OK.' He ground out his cigarette. 'Put 'em through.'

He picked up the phone, listened, and cut in. 'Are you saying that just because some kid—Yeah; I know it's the same kid but look—Yeah. Right. Have you any idea what's involved in mounting an operation of the kind you're proposing? D'you know how little time we have? That thing out there's already— Yeah. OK, OK. How soon will they be here? Right. Sure: I'll issue the necessary orders but I still think— Hello?' He gave a snort of frustration, slammed down the phone and glared at his Defence Chief.

'OK, Sam. Hold the missiles. Stay on Red Alert but don't launch. I'll get back to you later.' He dismissed the Chief with a wave and stabbed at the intercom. 'Get me Canaveral, Mary,' he snapped. 'And make it quick.'

*   *   *

As the President of the United States spoke to the Director of the launch-complex at Cape Canaveral, a car crossed Moscow's Red Square and turned in through an archway in the Kremlin wall. It carried the American Ambassador. It was followed seconds later by another, bearing his British counterpart. Within minutes the two men were in the private office of the President of Russia.

The President stood with his back to the ornate marble fireplace. His small eyes peered at the two diplomats from under bushy brows and his craggy features wore an expression of faint amusement.

'Well, gentlemen,' he purred. 'It is a strange world we live in. One minute, the three most powerful nations on Earth are squaring up to one another. Then a child in England speaks and we're friends again!' He shrugged. 'So: what can I do for you?'

The two men outlined the nature of the operation now being launched in their countries, and formally requested Russia's co-operation. The President had been briefed before their arrival and already knew everything they told him. When they had finished, he nodded.

'You may inform your respective Governments that Russia will co-operate in every way. This thing threatens the entire world, and so we must shelve our differences and work together.'

'That's right, sir,' said the American. 'We're all Earthmen now.'

The President shot him a quizzical look. 'I think,' he growled softly, 'that

144

you hope to get into the history books with that remark!'

'No, sir,' the man replied. 'What I do hope is that history won't end in about two days' time, when that thing out there decides to take breakfast!'

They shook hands, and minutes later two cars swept out of the Kremlin. Operation Egg-Blower was under way.

32

Brian came at dusk, and they went out into the garden to watch the show. Throughout the day, news bulletins had promised that it would be quite spectacular. The Earth, viewers and listeners had been told, was passing through a meteor-swarm. The meteors would do no damage, but as darkness fell they would become visible as countless points of light, drifting north-eastward. It would be as if the stars themselves were moving. Such a thing had never happened before in recorded history, and was unlikely to occur again within anyone's lifetime. Drivers were asked to pull over and park if they intended to watch the sky.

Orville, hands thrust deeply into the

pockets of his jeans, shivered. All up Prospect Place people were out. For them, it was a bit like Bonfire Night. Mrs Cashman had an ovenful of potatoes cooking in their jackets, and somebody further up had a tea-urn on a folding table. People moved up and down the Place, popping in and out of one another's houses; talking to neighbours they hadn't spoken to for years. And the scene, Orville knew, was being duplicated, over and over, across the night-side of the planet. It was all right for them.

He moved over to where the reporter stood, gazing into the darkening sky.

'Brian?'

'Aha?' Fox continued looking at the sky. His mouth was open.

'I'm sorry I shouted at you this morning. I was scared, that's all. I'm still scared.'

'So am I.' The reporter dropped his gaze, grinned and ruffled the boy's hair. 'Forget it, lad. Look at 'em out there; like an armada.' He looked up again, speaking in an awed whisper. 'A

147

space-armada, and you did it, lad. If it hadn't been for you, the generals and the flippin' scientists'd still be sitting on their backsides talking, and all these folk here would be inside watching telly and waiting to die. You've saved the lot of us, Orville; the whole damn world. D'you realize that?'

Orville shrugged, and shivered again. 'They haven't done it yet,' he said. 'It's a long way. That thing could be hatching out right now for all we know. I don't think I could eat one of Mrs Cashman's potatoes.'

Old McDougal appeared, carrying a tray. Brian shot Orville a warning glance and they rejoined his parents.

'Here y'are,' the old man said. 'Hot tea and biscuits.' He set the tray down on a rough bench by the hedge. The Copperstones smiled. Ever since the night of the storm, the old fellow had been casting about for something he might do for them. Orville wished for the hundredth time that he could tell him the truth.

They took mugs of tea and stood together, watching the stars. Presently, old McDougal began talking about the day long ago when, as a boy, he had watched a total eclipse of the sun through a bit of smoked glass. It was a sad story, Orville thought, because it had people in it who were dead now. It occurred to him that someday, many years from now, he would tell about tonight. Those he would tell were not born yet, and the people in the story, Mum and Dad, Brian and old McDougal, would be gone. He got an ache in his throat and swallowed, because he saw quite suddenly how sad it must be to be old.

The stars, drifting north-eastward, thinned like the end of a snowfall. Up the Place, people began moving indoors. Mr Copperstone looked at his watch. 'Eleven,' he said, then, for the old man's benefit, 'the best's over, I think. Shall we call it a day?'

'Aye.' Mr McDougal sighed, and turned to pick up the tray of empty mugs. Orville darted forward and took it.

'I'll bring it up for you,' he offered and, remembering the fragments on the old man's floor, added, 'I won't drop it.'

They went up towards McDougal's house. Mrs Cashman came down with salt and butter and spoons and they nodded, and said goodnight.

At the old man's door they stopped. Mr McDougal pushed it open and turned to take the tray. There was a tension between them; an awkwardness which Orville knew came from not being honest with his friend. He passed the tray carefully and mumbled, for the sake of something to say, 'Did you enjoy the meteors then, Mr McDougal?'

The crinkly eyes gazed so long into his own that he lowered them and the old man chuckled, drily.

'Meteors my foot,' he whispered.

Orville looked up, startled. Mr McDougal was turning, carrying the tray indoors. He paused and their eyes met.

'We all of us have things to do that aren't easy,' he said, softly. 'And to do them and keep quiet about them is the hardest thing of all. It takes a man.' He held the tray with one hand and reached for the door. 'Away with you, man; do what you have to do.'

The door closed. He stood a moment, staring at it. Then he turned and walked down towards home. Brian drove past and flashed his lights. Orville raised a hand. The car turned on to the main road and its engine noise faded to nothing. He looked up. The moving stars were gone. There were only the still ones now. A few hours and it would be over, one way or the other. Lights were going out all along the Place, and Orville knew they were going out everywhere else, too. He shivered. All those people going to sleep. Dreaming, perhaps; but never dreaming that there might be no tomorrow.

He went indoors. His father sat gazing at the newspaper before him on the table while his mother brewed tea in the kitchen. The radio played softly to itself on the coffee-table. Orville lowered himself into a chair and stared at the rug. Its pattern seemed to swim before his hot eyes and he closed them.

Time passed. The Earth was a grain of corn near a hungry bird and in the clock's loud tick he heard it coming: peck, peck, peck.

It rotated slowly in the blackness, so that all parts of its surface were warmed in turn by the sun.

Its incubation period was almost spent. Activity within had quickened. A crack had appeared close to its north pole and had lengthened, moving down across the equator and halfway to the southern pole.

Now the foetus rested, gathering strength for the last phase of its struggle to be born. Soon it would rouse itself, arch its neck and stretch out its limbs till the shell parted. It would emerge with the pain of hunger in its belly, to devour the star that warmed it. For the moment, though, it slept.

Silently, the ships of Operation Egg-Blower coasted in towards their target. All around them, nudged into initial motion by the tiny craft but now drifting free, floated a thousand chunks of space-debris. Great, empty fuel-tanks, each a hundred feet long, tumbled lazily, end-over-end like giant tin cigars. There were spent satellites and burnt-out third-stage boosters more than forty years old. Long-abandoned laboratories, their obsolete equipment stacked tidily, were dwarfed by the gleaming sails of solar-panels several miles across. Like a mass migration of assorted birds this motley armada flew towards the sun.

Commander Sam Wilbee squinted through his photochromic window and flicked a switch. 'All ships,' he rapped. 'This is Egg-Blower One. Distance from target, four-eighty thou. Earthtime 02.40. ETA 03.20. Stand by to switch to individual courses.'

In each ship, the astronavigator crouched over his miniature console and worked out his ship's new course. Every craft had been allocated a sector

154

of space and enough debris to fill it. Each ship carried an EV man who, at the proper time, would leave his craft and go to work outside, carrying cables across the void. EV was jargon for Extra-Vehicular. Chunks of debris would be tethered to the ships and the ships would tow them into position between the egg and the sun. Then, propelling themselves with air-bottles, the EV men would work among the debris, edging the pieces closer and closer together till they floated almost touching. There would be no need to fasten them, one to another. Placed in solar orbit and matching the speed of the egg, the hunks of metal would circle for ever. The barrier they formed would plunge the egg and its hideous occupant into cold, eternal night.

Wilbee's eyes swept the instrument-panel, flicked to the window, then back to the panel. The data was flashed to his brain, analysed and acted upon. His hands moved deftly over the controls. He spoke.

'All ships: this is Egg-Blower One. Distance from target four-forty thou.

Proceed independently. I repeat: proceed independently. Out.'

In response to his command, each crew moved smoothly into action. Airlock motors whined, hatches swung open and EV men emerged in their bulky suits. Steering themselves with squirts of air and paying out light cable from revolving drums on their belts, they crossed to the nearest chunks of debris and secured tow-lines. This done, they moved on to the next piece, and the next, until each ship towed behind it a string of assorted chunks. The E/Vs returned to their ships. Hatches were sealed. Steering motors flared briefly and the armada spread, each craft lugging its share of weightless metal towards its predetermined sector.

Three hundred and eight thousand miles away, the unborn creature stirred. Something, some instinctual sense flashed a warning to its awakening brain and it moved within the confines of its shell. The massive head turned, rubbing against the inner surface till it found the crack. An eyelid, sealed since the foetus was formed, split, and the thing looked for the first time on the universe of which it was a part.

Blackness, pricked with countless points of light. The eye relayed the picture to the brain, and the brain was quiet. This was right. And yet—

The egg rotated slowly. The eye peered out at the changing pattern of stars. A warning flared. The eye fastened on a cluster moving oddly; growing. The creature watched. The cluster spread. Individual points swelled, taking on shape. Rods and squares of light.

The beast was mindless, a hulk driven by instinct, and now that instinct recognized the enemy. It had no name for it. It only knew, with a dull, mindless sort of knowing, that the rods and squares were the work of the one force in the universe it feared: the force men called intelligence.

A million, million years this creature's ancestors had quartered the vastnesses between the stars; feeding, fighting, breeding. Unimaginably huge, they had swept the heavens, devouring stars and smashing everything in their path. And in all that time, they had encountered no force that could make them swerve, save one. Here and there, on tiny worlds in the rims of galaxies dwelt minute creatures which, multiplying with incredible speed, overspilled and spread out through nearby space, infecting other planets with their filth.

Minute, these creatures nevertheless possessed an awful power: power to construct objects very much bigger than themselves, and a billion times more strong. Objects that bore their tiny creators across the void and did their bidding. Their colonies were scattered thin across the heavens and they took on many forms, but all possessed this power that cancelled out their puny size and made them creatures to be feared.

So now the beast began struggling, its efforts fuelled by a fear learned over a thousand generations. They were coming; specks of life in bright machines, with powers beyond their size to outwit and confuse and destroy. It jerked back its head. It stretched out its talons and flexed its folded wings and heaved frantically. Along the egg's equator a fresh crack appeared. The creature heaved again and the crack zig-zagged west-to-east till it ran into the north-south fissure. A section of the shell lifted. Only strands of membrane held it now.

'For Chrissake, Skipper; look!'

Sam Wilbee winced at the shriek and flicked to transmit. 'Who are you?' he rapped. 'And what're we looking at?'

'Sorry, sir. Egg-Blower Four. Look at the egg, sir!'

Wilbee glanced through his window. The egg hung pale against the blackness. A section of the shell moved out and in like the gill of a fish.

'Hell!' He spoke rapidly into the mike. 'All ships. This is Egg-Blower One. E/Vs to operate with all speed: we have a problem!'

His headgear rang with exclamations in several languages as pilots watched the egg. The ships drifted, strung out in solar orbit, their hatches agape. All along the line, E/V men floated among the debris, jockeying gigantic lumps of metal into place. They heard their leader's order, glanced towards the egg and worked frantically, riding the lumps, propelling them with squirts of compressed air. The sun bathed the egg in light, warming it to life. They had minutes, an hour maybe, to get the hunks in place.

Slowly the shield took shape. A wall of metal, blazing silver on one side, coldly black on the other. On the eastern rim of the egg a shadow appeared. Slowly, as the E/Vs toiled, this shadow crept westward across the sunlit face. Within its shell, the creature felt it: a deathly, creeping chill. It fought; throwing itself in cramped desperation at the concave walls. The crack widened. Fresh ones appeared. Wilbee flicked a switch.

'All ships. Cut E/Vs adrift. Close hatches and activate steering-motors. Select debris-sections and ram. Push 'em into place, boys; time's running out.'

It was a desperate move. Pilots were

to cast off the lines which tied the E/V men to their ships, collide deliberately with chunks of floating debris and shove them into place. The E/Vs would be on their own, each man a tiny satellite. If an air-bottle gave out, a man might drift away from the fleet to circle the sun for ever. Or, manoeuvring tightly among the debris, a ship might strike one or catch him with a steering jet and roast him. All these things Sam Wilbee had considered in seconds. It was dangerous. Men and women might die. But then, if that thing got out of its shell they'd die anyway, and so would everyone else; the whole of humanity. There had been only one decision he could take. He called his own EV man.

'Sorry, Ed; I'm cutting you loose. G'luck!' All along the line, ships were casting off and closing their hatches. Steering motors flared. Ships' noses swung. Pilots peered out and selected their targets. A brief burst of power and a ship would go arrowing towards a fuel-tank or panel-sail. A touch of retro at the last second and the collision would be gentle; the target would float off, tumbling, in the right direction.

Far out on the edge of the operation, a man mistimed his break-burst. Ship and tank collided at speed. The ship ricocheted off, cartwheeling, its steering-motors gone. The pilot hit his transmit button. The radio was out. He activated the Mayday-beacon. Its sharp, urgent signal bleeped over every headphone in the fleet. Instantly, Wilbee cut in.

'Disregard Mayday,' he said flatly. 'Proceed with Operation.'

Nobody broke ranks. The stricken ship, distress-lights winking, spun away into the void. Its signal faded.

The fleet worked on. The shield lengthened and its shadow moved inexorably across the face of the egg. Wilbee touched a retro, blew a burnt-out booster gently at the E/V men and peered through his window. The egg was a half-moon, its eastern hemisphere blotted out. West of the shadow-rim, the shell-section still moved in and out like a gill. He watched. Was it his imagination, or were the creature's spasms weakening?

He screwed up his eyes against the glare. The thing was more than half eclipsed. It had to be feeling the cold by now; it had to be. The section of shell was almost detached and yet it was not moving as violently as before. As he watched it lifted: a great, triangular plate several miles across. The crack around it widened and the strands of membrane stretched, yet before it was stretched to its fullest extent, the movement ceased. Slowly, the plate sank back, like the last piece dropping into a jigsaw-puzzle. The cracks shrank to thin, zig-zag lines. There was no doubt about it: the thing was weakening. He nodded, breathed 'Yeah!' and flicked to transmit.

'All ships,' he said, coolly. 'This is Egg-Blower One. Target is dying. Keep it coming and we've got him cold. Out.'

They shuttled back and forth like bees. The mass of debris dwindled as the shield grew. The shadow moved across the egg and, with only a thin western crescent uneclipsed, the creature's movements ceased.

All along the line the crews went wild. Headsets crackled with laughter, cheers and bursts of song. Sam Wilbee, the professional, grinned wryly and called Earth.

'Houston; this is Egg-Blower One. Shield in position. Visible activity has ceased. Do instruments confirm? Over.'

Within hours of the egg's arrival in solar orbit, an instrument-package had been soft-landed on its surface and a team on Earth had monitored its readings ever since.

The voice of Houston responded at once and Wilbee heard its exultation through the static. 'Affirmative, Egg-Blower. Sub-surface temperature of target zero Celsius and falling. Instruments confirm cessation of life-processes. Out.'

In the privacy of his tiny cabin, Sam Wilbee permitted himself a second smile. 'OK, Houston.' He looked out. The little ships glinted like minnows in the sun. 'All right, boys,' he drawled. 'The party's over: let's go home.'

35

They kept the radio on all night. Just after six, a programme for farmers was interrupted for a newsflash. They tensed, goggling at one another through hot eyes. Was this it? Was this what each of them had prayed for, silently, over and over through the endless night? The reader's voice was cool; his delivery only faintly dramatic.

'We interrupt this programme to bring you a newsflash,' he said. 'At shortly after two a.m. BST today the combined space fleets of America and Russia successfully completed a massive operation in the vicinity of the mysterious planet which appeared recently in the Solar System. No details are yet available, but a Government spokesman told our reporter that by their courageous handling of a critical situation, the men and women of the combined fleets had averted a disaster of global proportions. We will of course let you have further details as they come to hand but in the meantime, back to *On Your Farm.*'

It was over. A normally undemonstrative family, they threw themselves on one another and clung together for a long time in the middle of the room. Mrs Copperstone cried, and started Orville crying too. Mr Copperstone, his arms tightly round them, rocked and mumbled, 'Thank God,' over and over.

It was the sound of a car outside which eventually separated them. They knew who it was before the knock came. Orville ran to open the door and Brian Fox strode in grinning.

'It's OK then!' he cried. 'Did you hear it?'

They told him they'd waited all night, listening for it. He sat down and waved an arm towards the still curtained window to indicate the world outside. 'There's nobody about,' he said. 'They're still asleep, the lot of 'em. It'd be just the same if the world had vanished: they wouldn't know any different!'

They laughed. 'It's not their fault, Brian,' said Orville. 'Nobody told 'em, did they? It was our secret and we kept it, too.' He felt like crying again. He had heard of people crying with joy and it had always sounded daft to him; like chuckling in agony. He knew what it meant now, though.

'Aye, well.' Brian clapped his hands together. 'They'll know now, soon enough. You'll be world-famous, lad; a celebrity. And quite right, too!'

Orville's blood froze. He stared at the reporter, aghast. Seeing his expression, Fox became serious.

'Hey; what's up, lad?' he said. 'It's bound to happen, y'know. You saved the world. You: not the combined fleets of whatever it was they said. If it hadn't been for you, the combined fleets would have been part of an early breakfast for that thing out there. You deserve to be famous, lad.'

Orville shook his head. 'I don't want to be, Brian. I don't like being looked at. Some people might like it, but I don't. I don't even like standing up in class at school. All those eyes, looking at you. Can't you stop it, Brian; please?' It would be bad enough as it was, going back to school next week. If he had to go back a celebrity he wouldn't be able to stand it. He'd have to run away.

Fox chewed his lip, gazing at the boy.

'I think he means it,' put in Mr Copperstone. 'He's a shy sort of lad, Brian; likes to keep himself to himself. Doesn't he, love?'

Orville's mother nodded. 'Yes.' Her voice was unsteady. 'There's no telling what it might do to him, Mr Fox, if all this gets out. Isn't there something you can do? We'd be ever so grateful.'

Fox shook his head. 'I don't know. I mean, now that it's over, somebody's going to give the whole story to the press. I don't know who that'll be, or I could ring and ask 'em to withhold Orville's name.' He was silent a moment, then he got up. 'Look,' he

169

said. 'I'll go down to the office and talk to a few people. Maybe somebody can tell me who to contact. I'll do my best anyway. You sit tight here and I'll let you know what happens. OK?'

*   *   *

It was all right. They never found out exactly how he did it, but when the story broke that day on a stunned population, there was no mention of Orville, or indeed of any boy at all. The impression was given that the scientists had found out what the mysterious planet was, and had devised Operation Egg-Blower as a way of dealing with it. For the next three days, Orville tuned in to every telecast with his fingers crossed, and Mr Copperstone bought the morning papers on his way to work. There was no mention. By the fourth day Orville felt easier. There'd be nothing now. His parents had felt sure somebody would remember his bit in the *Telegraph* and come sniffing round, but nobody did. Brian Fox had done it, and Orville felt a glow of gratitude for

170

his friend.

The holidays drew to a close. On the last Friday, Orville was sweeping out the loft when a car turned into Prospect Place and came bumping down over the cobbles. Orville heard it and, hoping it might be Brian, went and looked through the gateway.

The car was a gleaming black limousine. Brian was in it, but he wasn't driving. A man in a peaked cap was. There was somebody in the back with Brian, but Orville didn't know him.

The limousine drew up, and Orville felt a moment of panic. Had somebody found out? Were they here to take pictures and splash his face across the papers? He took a step backwards. At the first glimpse of camera or microphone he'd bolt for the loft and lock himself in.

The chauffeur got out, walked round the front of the car and opened the door. He never even glanced at Orville. Brian got out and turned to help the other man. They were lifting something between them. Orville watched closely, ready to run.

It was a basket. The chauffeur stepped forward, took it from them and placed it on the ground. It was quite a big basket, with ventilation spaces in it.

Brian glanced round, spotted Orville and beckoned. Orville approached the group uncertainly. He couldn't see any camera or anything, but what about the basket? Who was this man, and why had he come here in a posh, chauffeur-driven car? He was watching Orville and his face seemed kind, but he wasn't exactly smiling. The chauffeur just stood frosty-faced, looking at nothing. Orville stopped.

The dignified stranger gazed at him for a moment, and Orville gazed back. Then the man spoke, quietly, indicating the basket with a movement of his hand.

'I am commanded to thank you, Orville Copperstone,' he said. 'And to present to you this small gift, as thanks for what you have done. You are a brave and a modest young man.'

Orville looked down at the basket, then back at the man. He was too bewildered to speak. The man turned and spoke quietly to Brian, who smiled and nodded. The man turned, and the chauffeur held the door while he got back into the car. Then he strode round and got in himself. The engine purred, and the limousine backed slowly away up the Place, leaving only Brian and the basket.

Orville looked at the reporter. Brian grinned and touched the basket with his foot. 'Aren't you going to open it?' he asked.

Orville didn't move. His eyes followed the gleaming car as it swung out into the road and sped away. 'Who was that?' he whispered.

Brian laughed. 'You won't believe me when I tell you,' he said.

'Course I will,' the boy protested. 'Who?'

'That,' said Fox, 'was none other than the Royal Pigeon-Fancier.'

'Royal—' Orville's eyes narrowed. 'Are you kidding? Royal Pigeon-Fancier? I've never heard of him. You're having me on, aren't you?'

Brian shrugged. 'I told you you

wouldn't believe me. He's the Royal Pigeon-Fancier and he lives at Sandringham. He looks after the Queen's pigeons. Open the basket.'

Orville's heart was thumping. He knelt down by the basket, lifted the lid and gasped. There, blinking on a bed of straw, sat two magnificent birds. He reached out a hand, slowly, touching the sleek, perfect feathers. 'Oh, Brian,' he breathed. 'These are Doridins.' His throat ached suddenly and he felt tears on his face. 'I don't believe it,' he whispered. 'I just don't believe it!' For the second time that week, Orville was crying with joy.

*   *   *

When Mr McDougal had been fetched, and the Doridins handled, cooed over and introduced to their new home, Brian left. His car was back at the office and he'd have to walk. Still, he told himself, there might easily have been no world left to walk in. He grinned, remembering Orville's face when he first saw his Doridins, and

174

went whistling up the Place.

He had just turned into the main road when a voice piped, 'Hey, mister!' He turned and saw two little girls whose faces looked vaguely familiar. One of them had a fat plastic carrier which she held out to him. 'Here.' Her face was red and she was looking very pleased with herself. 'You said you saved them so we've been collecting them for you. Haven't we, Sarah?'

Fox looked in the carrier. It was crammed with about two thousand toffee-wrappers. He looked at the girls with his mouth open. They smiled.

'I bet nobody's got a collection as big as yours now,' said Sarah. 'Nobody in the world!'

Fox gazed down into the sticky bag. 'No,' he admitted, gloomily. 'I bet they haven't, at that.'

Monday morning. Twenty-to-nine, and the end of the holidays. Orville dawdled along the road. Two boys overtook him on bikes. One of them said something to the other and they both laughed. Orville felt that ache he always felt when people laughed that way. He hadn't heard what the boy had said but he knew it had been about him. He sighed, thinking about the playground and the long term ahead.

It could all have been different of course. If he'd not got Brian to stop the publicity he'd be famous. Orville: the boy who saved the world. He could still make it happen, too, if he wanted. He had only to phone some newspaper and tell his story and bingo! They'd stop laughing at him then all right. They'd have to.

There'd probably be a sort of ceremony in the hall, with him up on the platform with Mr Magson and Mr McPhee. The Governors would be there of course, and probably the Lord Mayor. He pictured the boys, row upon row, gazing up from the floor of the hall as he received a certificate, a cheque for one thousand pounds and a medal. Mr Magson would make a speech. Orville could see him now, ramrod-straight, glaring down at the boys with his hands on the lapels of his jacket.

'Never before in the history of this school,' he would say, 'has a member of the second year become Head Boy. Today, therefore, we are gathered here to witness a little bit of history being made.' At this point, the Headmaster would turn towards Orville, standing modestly on one side.

'Orville Copperstone,' he would say. 'We hereby appoint you Head Boy, with all the privileges and responsibilities that post entails. It is the very least we can do.'

'Hey, Coppers!'

He came out of his dream with a start. He had reached the school gates without noticing, and Dean Foulger was lounging there with his hands in his pockets. Dean Foulger was one of daft Cowling's hangers-on. He had pale, curly hair and a high voice and if it hadn't been for Cowling the others would have given him a rough ride. He called out tauntingly to Orville. 'What did you do in the hols, eh, Coppers?' A knot of boys hung around the gateway. They looked at Orville; ready for a laugh. Orville felt himself going red.

'I saved the world,' he imagined himself saying. 'I saved you, Foulger, and your rotten boss, Cowling, too. I had to, because you're all part of the world and there's some good things in the world, too.'

He could have said that. He nearly did, but then he remembered what Mr McDougal had said the other night. 'We all of us have things to do that aren't easy,' he had said. 'And to do them and keep quiet about them is the hardest thing of all. It takes a man.'

He looked into Foulger's mocking eyes and answered quietly, knowing what would happen. 'I got a pair of Doridins, Foulger.'

'Doridins!' The word burst from twenty eager throats and Foulger, flapping his arms like wings, ran off shrieking into the playground to tell Cowling.